THE LONELY PLAINS

The Lonely Plains

Esther Loewen Vogt

HORIZON HOUSE PUBLISHERS
CAMP HILL, PENNSYLVANIA

Horizon House Publishers
3825 Hartzdale Drive
Camp Hill, PA 17011

ISBN: 0-88965-100-0
LOC Catalog Card Number: 92-75484
© 1993 by Horizon House Publishers
Printed in the United States of America

93 94 95 96 97 5 4 3 2 1

Cover illustration by Brenda Wintermyer
Cover design by Step One Design

Dedication

To my sister Ruth Loewen who is a lover of books, a former librarian and a firm follower of Jesus Christ.

AUTHOR'S NOTE

*F*or readers like me who like to have the fact and fiction sorted out, I offer the following:

In Captain Zebulon Pike's *Journal of the Western Expedition* published in 1810, Americans caught their first glimpse of trade with the Spanish Southwest when the historic Santa Fe Trail opened the door.

Over the 800 mile Trail that crossed Kansas came traders, freighters, soldiers, buffalo hunters, pioneers and gold seekers. Some found fame and fortune; others only death on the lonely plains. For over 50 years travel continued along this wide "highway" that helped the westward push in the United States.

Independence, Missouri, became the eastern terminus of the Trail. From Westport Landing (now a part of Kansas City) the Trail snaked across Kansas via Council Grove, the last "civilized outpost" as it was called, to its destination of Santa Fe, New Mexico. Freighters moved tons of goods in wagons down this trail. One firm employed 5,000 men and used 3,500 wagons, moving 16,000,000 pounds of freight in 1866. Stage coaches and wagon trains also used the Trail on their trek West. Because of the Indian menace in the western half of Kansas, forts sprang up to protect the travelers and to provide army escorts for caravans.

In *The Lonely Plains*, Barbara and Charlie head for the Pawnee Rock/Fort Larned area to live on their homestead. Few settlers had taken up claims here, and the treeless plains stretched far west, dotted here and there with a lone sodhouse or a dugout.

In my old Kansas history book, I boned up on Pawnee Rock, one of the most dangerous places for surprise Indian attacks along the Trail. Indians hid behind this actual sandstone formation to attack travelers. Fort Larned was deactivated in July, 1878, but exists as a museum today. Forts Zarah and Harker vanished as the need for soldier protection diminished.

Steamboat travel along the Missouri River was prominent until the railroads were laid across Missouri and later in Kansas. Hermann, a German town on its Missouri "Rhine" had a steamboat industry. Barbara's visit provides a bit of background from the paddle wheel days.

When Barbara and her Cousin Bitsy arrive in Atlanta in 1866, they're appalled by the destruction of the southern city, but notice how it is being rebuilt. I wrote to Atlanta's Historical Society and asked for information about the city during 1866. They sent generous copies of pages of history following the Civil War. I received information telling of businesses, depots, homes, hotels and even the baseball team being rebuilt after the war.

Dr. Griffin was head of the smallpox hospital at the time. The Tullie Smith Plantation and the Presbyterian church with Pastor Mallard were factual too.

The Ohio-Kentucky Railroad was apparently spared from Yankee destruction and I learned that it went north into Illinois then west to St. Louis. Later railroads crossed Missouri into Kansas.

Although Merritt Wallace is a fictional character, Bluemont College in Manhattan has gone on to become Kansas State University.

I have tried to portray this era of Kansas and Atlanta history in 1866 through Barbara's eyes. If it has deviated from fact, it

is no less stranger than the facts themselves which were
sometimes vague and unclear in my research. Thus, this
novel is a work of fiction, but it is based on fact and used
fictiously.

Esther Loewen Vogt
Hillsboro, Kansas

Santa Fe Trail

Kansas
(1866)

- Westport Landing (Now Kansas City)
- Council Grove
- Marion Centre
- Cottonwood Crossing
- Ellsworth
- Warren's Soddy
- Pawnee Rock
- Fort Larned

To Colorado

To Santa Fe, New Mexico

*"No one who puts his hand to the plow
and looks back is fit for service
in the kingdom of God."*
(Luke 9:62)

CHAPTER 1

*T*he day had dawned clear and brittle. Although rain had fallen the night before, it was a sudden, squally rain that had cleansed and refreshed the late summer landscape.

Barbara Temple stood in the doorway of her Uncle Daniel Moore's log cabin and gazed across the undulating prairies to the south. The morning was golden, and sunshine flowed like honey from the pale August sky. *My wedding day,* she thought with a catch in her throat. *Mine and Charlie's, to be held in Marion Centre's new log church.* She smiled a little, rather surprised at the sudden turn of events of the past week.

Charlie Warren and his 11-year-old brother, Willie, had worked for days to outfit the schooner that would take them about 90 miles west of Marion Centre. Living on the rich, bottom land that summer of 1865 had left a bad taste in Charlie's mouth when the sleepy Cottonwood River had raged out of it banks following a heavy downpour and swept away everything he owned. With Kansas weather, anything could happen.

"How could I have hated Charlie?" Barbara muttered aloud. Her thoughts drifted back over the past two years. *At first, I thought he was rude and brash. Then my heart began to change as I began to appreciate him for the man he was. When I learned he and Willie were moving west, I knew I loved him. I realized I wouldn't have all the time in the world to show him how I felt. That's when I told him I wanted to go with him.* "As his wife," she murmured softly under her breath.

"What did you say, Barbie?" Her cousin Bitsy swooped up from behind with her fat, yellow braids flying. "You're not having famous last thoughts about marrying Charlie Warren, are you? To leave the groom at the altar? I thought you had finally grown to love him!"

Barbara shook her head until her thick, chestnut hair tumbled down her back. "Oh, I do! But it's not at all the way I'd always dreamed—"

"Let's see . . . I bet you planned a pink and white ceremony under a shower of magnolia blossoms and an army of attendants. Well, instead you came out to Kansas. Was it only two years ago? Then you fell in love with our prairies. You know, I was petrified you wouldn't realize you loved Charlie until it was too late."

"I almost didn't, did I?" Barbara said with a wry smile. "Yes, I'd always planned a fancy wedding to Matthew Potter on the wide sweep of lawns of our plantation back in Georgia, until the war came and messed everything up. When Father was killed, Mother lost the plantation. Fortunately for me your father offered me a home here, after she died."

Her lustrous blue eyes grew dreamy, remembering. It hadn't been easy, leaving her old home and friends in the South and coming to Kansas to live with her mother's brother Daniel Moore and his family. He and Aunt Prudy and five lively cousins had welcomed her with open arms. The fact that she was a Rebel and Uncle Daniel's family were Yankees hadn't made it any easier. In fact, it had grated harshly for so long. Now the war was finally over, and North and South were becoming a Union once more. Through the difficult war years Barbara's values had changed.

"Frankly, Barbie, at first I couldn't *stand* you! I thought you were a snob," Bitsy snorted. A pout framed her piquant face. "But you came to your senses, and so did we. Now you couldn't be dearer to me than if you were my own sister. Know something? I'm gonna miss you terribly!"

Barbara saw tears lurking in Elizabeth's baby-blue eyes. She threw out her arms and hugged her cousin tightly. "Oh, Bitsy!"

The two girls clung to each other briefly, then Bitsy stepped back from Barbara and walked toward the open doorway.

"Well, you're the bride and I have flowers to pluck for your wedding bouquet, not to mention a garland to weave for your hair. No magnolia blossoms, I'm afraid, Barbie. It would serve Charlie right if I fixed him a boutonniere of poison oak for dragging you out to the wilds of the West."

"Considering it was you who shoved me into Charlie's arms in the first place," Barbara snorted.

"Oh, come now, Barbie. You know I carried a torch for him until I saw he had eyes for no one but *you*. You were pining for him after Matthew Potter was killed. Lucky you realized it was Charlie you loved all along. It was written all over you."

With a sudden twirl, Bitsy rushed from the cabin and disappeared down the path that led toward the river.

A smile tugged at Barbara's lips at the thought of Bitsy's words. They were true. She and Matthew had planned to be married after the war was over. Her world had crashed when word came that he had been killed in battle. How she had railed and ranted against God! Even when Charlie began showing attention to her, she had rebelled. But through the love of Uncle Daniel and his family, God had shown her He was in control. That's when she had surrendered her will to Him. Far too long she had been selfish and arrogant, a snob, a prissy Southern belle. She had disdained the love and the home that her uncle and his family had offered her, until she learned that she was much more precious to God than she had thought possible. Her appreciation for the Moores and others, like Charlie, had grown after God worked a change in her heart.

When she was afraid Charlie would go West without her, she knew she'd be losing not only a wonderful prospect for a husband, but also his brother who had become her best friend. She couldn't let him go because at the last minute she discovered she *did* love him.

Turning away from the door she ran her fingers through her thick chestnut hair. She had washed it last night and now it curled in soft tendrils around her face. Glancing in the crooked mirror above the apple crate washstand, she studied her reflection: her lustrous, deep-blue eyes like her mother's, her unimportant nose, her too-thin mouth, her determined chin. She didn't look much different than she had two years ago; yet she had changed more than she thought possible, especially after she had asked Jesus Christ to live in her heart just a few months before.

I wonder if Aggie has ironed my old green bombazine, she thought suddenly. Instead of a dainty, lace-tiered, ruffled wedding gown of white, watered silk, she had no choice but to wear a dress she'd worn many times before. There wasn't time nor money for a beautiful bridal gown.

Just then her cousin Aggie scrambled from the loft with the soft, green dress flung over her arm.

"Oh, Barbara," Aggie chirked, "I just tacked a lace ruching around the neckline. It perks it up a bit. Sorry I couldn't whip up something new for the occasion. You didn't give me enough time."

"I know, and it's sweet of you, Aggie, about the lace. But no, there wasn't time nor money for a new wedding dress. Charlie and I are lucky to be married in a church."

"You're a brave woman, Barbara," Aggie said. "Not only brave, but very pretty. I hope Charlie Warren appreciates the precious cargo he's taking down the Santa Fe Trail. If you can survive a soddy after being raised in a large plantation house—"

"I know it won't be easy," Barbara cut in, fingering the full skirt of the fine silken twill. "But I love Charlie. Somehow, with God's help, we'll make it."

"Bravo! A year ago I would've thought you were crazy if you'd said so, but today I believe you really mean it." Aggie shook out the dress and held it up. "See? It doesn't look too bad, does it? And the color's perfect for you. That green goes well with your hair and your coloring." She moved toward the table and laid down the dress.

"Thanks again, Aggie, for all you've done," Barbara said in a low voice. "I don't know how I could have made it without you . . . any of you!"

The tepid August air hung like a limp sheet over the hot kitchen as Aggie picked up the flat iron and moved it carefully over the delicate fabric.

"Better make sure your trunk is packed," Aggie said in her usual commanding, brusque way, whisking the iron over the full skirt. If we'd known about the wedding a month ago, I could've stitched up an extra set of sheets and pillow cases. Make sure Charlie and Willie bring all their belongings from their cabin."

"I'm sure they've packed all that's worth taking. As for a dowry . . . I guess I never really thought about that. When your sister Vange got married, you did it up properly and beautifully. I wouldn't expect—"

"Why not? You're one of us, aren't you?" Aggie's words were clipped. "And don't you ever forget it! Now, upstairs with you to finish packing. In another hour we'll head for the church."

Barbara never knew where the time flew once she scurried up the loft. She finally closed her little trunk with a thump and paused to look around the tiny bedroom she had shared with her cousins since her arrival in late June of 1863. She remembered the many times the yellow cowslip moon had peeped through the small east window of the loft for a gentle goodnight, and the warm, feather ticks that had kept off the cold, winter winds as the girls had snuggled together under the mound of bedclothes. She would miss them so much! Then Charlie's handsome face with his dark curls and crooked grin flashed before her, and she knew the choice she had made was right.

"Barbara!" Aggie's voice called up to her. "Are you ready for my help with your wedding finery?"

She drew a quick breath and nodded. "As ready as I'll ever be."

Aggie scrambled up the ladder with the freshly pressed green bombazine and slipped it lightly over Barbara's head. She patted the moss-green velvet bows on the shoulders, then tied the wide sash in the back. *Dear Aggie,* Barbara thought, *what would I ever have done without her?*

Plain, capable, calm and sensible with freckles like speckled turkey eggs and mousy-brown hair twisted into a taut bun on her neck, Aggie Moore was one person upon whom everyone could depend. Barbara suspected she sacrificed herself for her family because she needed people to make her happy.

Aggie's beautiful sister, Evangeline, known as Vange, had once said in admiration of Aggie that "she could make a meal out of cornstalks and whip up a ball gown out of half a flour sack." That was an understatement, Barbara decided. When Vange had married Barry Keaton last spring, it was Aggie who had undertaken the gigantic job of putting together the bride's trousseau. Mammy Crissy from the plantation couldn't have done a better job than Aggie Moore. And that assessment coming from the Southern belle herself, made Barbara recall how she had come to appreciate Aggie, too.

"Well, I think you're ready, Barbara," Aggie said after she had ratted and patted Barbara's hair once more. "Except for the garland of flowers Bitsy is fixing. Step carefully when you go down the ladder. We don't want you to trip and break a leg on your wedding day. Although if it would delay your departure—"

"Never mind. I've learned to maneuver the ladder as well as any of you, after all this time!"

As Barbara let herself down cautiously, Aunt Prudy's tiny figure emerged from the small, east bedroom, wearing her usual shiny, black "company" dress. The sparse, gray topknot perched like a bump on a log on the top of her head, and her blue-gray eyes crinkled into a smile when she saw Barbara.

"You look right pert, child," she exclaimed. "As beautiful a bride as ever walked the earth." Then she grew solemn. "My dear, it won't be easy to let you go, after you've been a part of us these two years. I . . ." She paused to take off the wire-rimmed spectacles and wiped her eyes with the corner of a white handkerchief. "I hope you know how much we'll miss you!"

Tears stung Barbara's eyes at Aunt Prudy's words. It wouldn't be easy to leave the comfortable log cabin with all its homey things and dearly familiar furnishings. *And to think,* she reminded herself, *that two years ago I would've jumped at the chance to chuck it all.*

Without a word she flung her arms around the tiny woman and hugged her. "Oh, Aunt Prudy, you'll never know how I'll miss you! But I love Charlie, and I must go where he goes."

"Of course, child. That's how it should be. You know, 'Whither thou goest I will go . . . ,' like the Scriptures say. It's time to climb aboard the wagon. Pa's already out front with the team. Let Josh help you up, and don't crush those ruffles when you sit down. Aggie's spent an hour pressing your gown."

Barbara stepped carefully from the south door of the cabin where Uncle Daniel waited with Pet and Polly and the wagon. Her cousin Joshua hobbled out to meet her.

He gave a low whistle and bowed dramatically. "Allow me, Madame. I'll hoist your Prairie Highness up on the seat beside Pa. Bitsy will have to squat in back with her basket of blooms, if she ever gets here with them."

Josh humped slightly as he placed his arms around her waist and helped her over the wagon wheel. He didn't let the loss of a leg stop him from anything.

"Thank you, Josh. You're one of the most gallant men I've ever met." she said quietly. "You know I'll miss you dreadfully."

"Then you've forgiven me for being a Yankee soldier instead of a Reb?" he bantered, swinging her carefully onto the wagon seat.

"The war is over now. Life is changing for us all." She couldn't think of anything funny to say.

"That it is, Cousin. That it is."

At that moment Bitsy rushed from the woods, her arms

loaded with a basket of cascading fall flowers. Long spires of blue lupine, bunches of Indian paintbrush, tall stems of bright yellow sunflowers and branching clusters of goldenrod spilled over the brim of woven wicker as she hurriedly stashed them on the rear of the wagon.

"I hunted everywhere . . . Barbie," she panted. "But all I could find . . . for your hair were a few prairie lilies. I looked for some wild columbine, but I guess they're bloomed out."

"Count yourself lucky that she didn't include wild onions or snakeroot," Josh snorted.

"I'm not as stupid as that, dear brother," Bitsy murmured sweetly.

"Maybe not. If you were, I'd have gone for some of that smartweed for you. I saw some down by the Cottonwood. That would've been fittin'."

Before Bitsy could form a cutting response, Aunt Prudy and Aggie slammed the south door of the cabin and joined the others on the wagon. Soon it lumbered down the dim trail toward town. Already the vivid green of summer had given way to the deeper green of August, and the team kicked up skiffs of dust as the wheels rolled toward Marion Centre.

CHAPTER 2

*B*arbara strained her eyes for Charlie's team as they neared the log church. Their plans had been made so hastily that she realized she really knew very little about her future husband. But it wasn't as though Charlie hadn't *tried* to get to know her better. She recalled his attempts at the Fourth of July picnic and the box lunch social, and how she had spurned him.

She knew more about his brother, Willie, than she did about Charlie. She had met Willie when she'd wandered out to the Cottonwood River one day almost two years ago. Willie had reminded her so much of her brother, Whatley, who was about the same age when he died a few years earlier. Willie's freckle-spattered face, tousled hair and friendly ways filled her life with a brotherly sort of joy that she had missed. When Willie lay deathly ill with diphtheria, she had nursed him through the worst of it. How concerned Charlie had been for her at the time, yet she rejected his concern as a sign of brashness! Now she would really get to know Charlie—as her husband.

Willie had told her of the time the Warrens had started out from Illinois in their covered wagon. Renegade Indians in Missouri had killed their parents and their sister, Nellie May. There was nothing left for Willie and Charlie to do but to come to Kansas and prove the claim their father had pre-empted. But although the claim took in the rich bottom land, a heavy rain had swept away all the crops and Charlie's precious flock of sheep a few weeks ago. That's when he and Willie decided to move away from the Cottonwood River and go farther west. For so long Charlie had tried to win Barbara's love, but she had resented the brash attentions of the young "sheepman," as she had called him—until she discovered she really did love him. When she wasn't able to talk them out of leaving, she decided to marry Charlie and go West with him and Willie.

She had not regretted her hasty decision, but everything had happened so quickly that she wasn't quite ready to relinquish the growing Marion Centre settlement along the Cottonwood so abruptly. Had she really hated the prairie when she came? Funny how it had become so interwoven with her life here. So much had happened since her grief over Matthew's death and her eventual acceptance of Uncle Daniel's God for herself on this prairie.

The wagon pulled to a stop under the grove of walnut trees near the church. Already buckboards and horses were tied to the hitching rack, for this was to be one of the first weddings in the newly organized congregation. Charity Shreve had told her that the Quaker elder would be on hand for the church dedication, and could perform the ceremony.

Just then she heard a familiar whinny, and she turned her head. Charlie rode up beside the wagon. The dark curls over his broad forehead and his incredibly blue eyes shone in the warm August afternoon. He slid from his horse and reached out his hand to help her from the wagon, then gently drew her toward him, pushed back the fringe of her brown hair, and kissed her softly on the lips.

"Barbara," his voice was low and husky, "Barbara, my darling. I wanted to be sure I wasn't dreaming, and you're really going to marry me!"

"Yes," she whispered, looking deeply into his eyes. "Oh, yes, Charlie! It's amazing, but it's true. Is Willie here?" she added anxiously.

"I told him to make sure he'd scrubbed his face. I won't have him embarrass you with egg on his mouth."

Bitsy was tugging at her sleeve. "The wedding can't start until the bride is ready. Here I roam all over the prairies to find flowers for a wreath for her hair, and I find her kissing the first man who lures her from the wagon! Charlie, why don't you look up Elder Buck? Make sure he's broken in his new boots. They squeaked something fierce at Vange's wedding last spring."

"I'll trot back to the cabin for skunk oil if they do," Aggie offered as she picked an armload of flowers and hurried into the church. Willie, with his face scrubbed and hair neatly combed, hovered around like a stray pup, and meekly followed Aggie inside the church. Barbara caught the pleased smile in his eyes as he glanced back at her.

Bitsy set a garland of prairie blooms on Barbara's head and thrust a bouquet into her arms. The little church was already rapidly filling with guests, and Uncle Daniel touched Barbara's arm before entering the church.

"Barbara, you're a real credit to your mother. If she could look down from heaven and see her sweet-faced, clear-eyed young daughter . . ." He paused to look for Charlie who had come back to take Barbara's arm.

"Uncle Daniel," Barbara's voice was thick with tears, "If I'm sweet-faced and clear-eyed, it's because you didn't give up on me!" She noticed the faraway look in his deep-blue eyes that she would never forget. "I just wanted to say . . . thank you! I'll always remember the day you picked me up at Council Grove . . . and I was upset because you didn't come in a carriage . . ." A sob broke into her words.

Bitsy twined the last of the prairie lilies into Barbara's hair and eyed her with a critical glance.

"You'll do, Barbie. Charlie, if you don't take proper care of this gorgeous creature, I'll send Captain Blake from Fort Riley to kidnap her back home. And I mean it!"

"Don't worry, Bitsy. I promise I'll make her so happy she'll never want to leave our soddy! And now I think it's time we meet Elder Buck in front of the church."

Slowly he took Barbara's arm and led her toward the doorway. Bitsy scrambled ahead of them and almost flew down the aisle with a twirl of her pink, chambray skirts.

With her eyes on Charlie's face, Barbara walked beside him toward the crude pulpit in the dimly lit log church. The scent of fresh-hewn logs mingled with the aroma of prairie flowers that banked the small puncheon platform. As she moved slowly down the aisle, Barbara saw the familiar faces of the Shreves, the Billings and the other settlers who had become so dear to her. It would be hard to leave it all. Willie fidgeted on the split log bench beside Uncle Daniel and Aunt Prudy and her cousins near the front. They were all the "family" she had.

The Quaker elder waited for them, his lined face solemn and kind. When Barbara and Charlie paused before him, he opened his Bible. Clearing his throat, he read several Scriptures and without another word, he plunged into the vows.

"Does thee, Charles Warren, take Barbara Temple to be thy lawful wedded wife, to love and to cherish, in sickness and in health, as long as thee both shall live?"

"I do." Charlie's voice rang out firm and clear.

"Does thee, Barbara Temple, take Charles Warren to be thy lawful wedded husband, to love and to cherish, to be faithful—on the Santa Fe Trail and on the wide plains—in sickness and in health, as long as thee both shall live?"

For a moment Barbara caught her breath at the strange phrasing that had crept into the elder's vows. *Now why would he have included those striking words?* she wondered. With a quick gulp Barbara nodded. "Yes, yes, I will." She knew that it was forever with Charlie, wherever God led.

As they knelt on the dirt floor for the blessing, Barbara felt a quiet peace steal over her, and she raised her head and looked at Charlie. He seemed so solemn and sober that she knew he felt the same.

When she lifted her face for his kiss of commitment, Barbara knew this was the nearest thing to heaven on earth she had experienced. If her heart could hold any more joy it would burst, she was sure.

An hour later Barbara and Charlie were at Uncle Daniel's

cabin with their covered wagon backed up to the south door. On the shelves Charlie had built along the inside of the wagon, Aunt Prudy was loading smoked hams, slabs of bacon, sacks of carrots, new potatoes, jugs of molasses, canned goods, garden seeds and a pile of comforters and quilts.

"I want to send you off on a good start," she said when Barbara remonstrated. "I did this for Rosie and John, and for Vange and Barry. I'd do the same for all my children. You're as dear as any one of them. Besides, you have an extra mouth to feed with Willie. Here's a wild rosebush I dug out by the river. Be sure to plant it beside your soddy when you get there, and keep it well-watered."

Barbara, her heart full of love and emotion, could scarcely speak. Now that the time for leave-taking had come she felt suddenly afraid. *Had she been too hasty? Could she have talked Charlie and Willie into staying here?*

She cried when she bid her uncle and aunt and cousins goodbye. *My family* she reminded herself. *At least I know they're standing by us, with their love and prayers.* The 90 miles seemed like a million miles away.

Then she gave her head a sharp toss and jutted out her chin. She had weathered other traumatic situations with God's help, and she would make it now, too.

As Charlie hoisted her onto the wagon seat, Barbara's gaze strayed to the west where the dim, rutted road crept through the tall, prairie grasses and led into the flaming sunset. Willie's horse pranced impatiently beside the wagon.

Just then Aggie's slight figure, still in its brown alpaca, flew to the wagon. In her hands she carried a perky, bright percale bonnet. She thrust it into Barbara's lap.

"For you," she said with a breathless laugh. "No pioneer woman rides off into the sunset with only prairie lilies in her hair." With a quick nod, Barbara removed the garland of lilies and tossed it to Bitsy. Then she jammed the bonnet on her head and tied it firmly under her chin.

"Thank you, Aggie. I'll need it. Even if I vowed I'd never wear one of these."

Bitsy tried to tide over Barbara's discomfort of leaving as she placed the garland on her blond head and struck a statuesque pose to catch Barbara's eye. When she was sure she had Barbara's attention, she broke into an impossibly high-pitched, tuneless ballad:

"Bonnie Charlie's going away
Safely over the friendly main.
Many a heart will break in twain—"

The song broke off suddenly with Bitsy's sob. With a firm thrust of her chin, Barbara turned her gaze away and looked at Charlie as she waited for him to cluck to the team.

CHAPTER 3

"*W*hen the road reaches Cottonwood Crossing we'll travel west before nightfall," Charlie said as the wagon creaked slowly toward the northwest the next morning. "We'll pick up the Santa Fe Trail there." He paused, then leaned toward Barbara. "Tired, darling? We had a long, hard day yesterday."

Barbara adjusted the ties of her sunbonnet. "I'm fine, Charlie. I guess it's because I'm so happy with you—and Willie. He's doing a good job, riding herd on the four cows, isn't he?"

"He's the 'bullwhacker'! He insisted that wrangling was his job. And that my place was beside my wife."

Wife! Barbara savored the word like a ripe strawberry. They had spent the night in Charlie's almost empty cabin in the glen. Willie had crawled promptly into his built-in bed in the curtained ell. As Charlie had said, it had been a long, tiring day with the wedding and the last minute packing all rolled into one. But they were up early and with only the bedding and a few dishes from a hurried breakfast to load into the wagon, they had left at daybreak.

She vowed she'd never leave Charlie, no matter if they traveled to the ends of the earth. How could she ever have hated him? Perhaps Willie had helped make up her mind as he constantly quoted his big brother. Once she'd grown tired of his "Charlie says," until she learned that Charlie was all Willie claimed he was.

At noon they had stopped in the shade of a lone elm— "nooning," Willie had called it. They ate some of Aggie's dried apple pies and beaten biscuits and munched on slices of cold fried ham packed in the wicker basket.

The sun was now below the horizon and the red glow faded into pink as the stillness of the prairie crept over the countryside.

"That is where we join the Trail up ahead," Charlie said suddenly, pointing to a wooded blur beside the road. "We'll stop for camp under the clump of trees."

When the wagon crawled toward the campsite, purple twilight melted into darkness. One ray of pale gold shimmered far along the zenith and lost itself in the deepening dusk. The trail to the northwest was a dull line against the dark prairies.

Stopping beneath the cluster of trees, the wagon wheels seemed to sigh with the whisper of the evening breeze. In minutes Willie had gathered wood for a fire while Charlie staked out the horses and cows. Tied beneath the wagon, a crate of Aunt Prudy's hens crooned their nighttime chants as crickets fiddled and creaked in the bushes.

Barbara took the large iron skillet from the wagon and rummaged for eggs and bacon. She found the gray enameled coffee pot and a pan of Aggie's cornbread. When the fire burned briskly she began to prepare the evening meal.

I must be careful not to scorch anything this time, she mused, remembering her devastating efforts to prepare breakfast the morning John and Rosie's baby, Sammie, was born while her cousins took care of the morning chores. Who would have dreamed a year ago that she would fix a campfire supper now! The aroma of frying bacon and bubbling coffee drifted over the quiet evening air, and darkness crowded against the pitiful circle of light cast by the smoking, spitting fire.

Soon Willie and Charlie came out of the darkness and sat

by the fire. Willie had milked the cows and strained the milk. There was plenty to drink. Barbara piled the tin plates high with bacon and eggs and set out slabs of cornbread. She had found a jar of Aunt Prudy's dills and a pat of rather squishy butter among the staples on the wagon shelves.

"Boy, this is great, Barbara!" Willie said, smacking his lips. "Ever since you and me gathered them walnuts and baked those yummy cookies you've been cookin' real good, Bitsy told me."

Barbara laughed. "It took me a long time to learn. I grew up not knowing how to do a thing. We had Mammy Crissy and Mammy Louisy and their kitchen help to do the work, so why should I? But now . . . " She spread out her hands helplessly.

"Now you have us, Barbara," Charlie said softly, wiping the last crumb of egg from his plate with a crust of cornbread. "Willie and I have cooked for ourselves for a long time. If you ever run into a bind, just let us know."

"Once we get to our soddy, it'll be easier to cook," Willie added. "I'm glad Charlie found that little topsy stove for cookin'."

"So am I," Barbara said. "Except, what do we do for fuel on the flat plains without trees for wood?"

Willie and Charlie looked at each other. In the dim firelight Barbara notice their whimsical glances. Finally Charlie spoke.

"Prairie coal."

"P-prairie coal?"

"More simply said, buffalo chips," he added.

"Buffalo chips!" Barbara screeched. "You mean we burn that stuff?"

"Sure. Why not? God provided manna for the Israelites and He also provides our fuel. I'll make sure to gather a good supply each day," Willie cracked.

For a long time Barbara stared at the glimmering fire. There was still so much she hadn't thought about when she had promised to go West with Charlie. Sure, they were moving only some 90 miles away, but she had heard that the Kansas territory was flat and treeless beyond the horizon.

"At least our soddy has a wooden floor," Charlie said. "So many dugouts and sodhouses are packed with dirt. When Ike Courtney said he'd trade claims with me I told him there was only one stipulation: that the house have a floor. It has two rooms, he says. Even a tiny cellar."

"It . . . it sounds n-nice," Barbara squeaked. "I . . . I'm sure I can make it homey."

The pale-yellow cowslip prairie moon swung up into the dark sky and Willie yawned. Barbara had flung her sunbonnet aside and began to unplait her long brown hair.

Charlie picked up her hand gently. "You're tired, too. It's time to turn in." Then he drew a small leather bound Bible from his pocket, paged through the Psalms and read one verse aloud.

"The Lord is my light and my salvation; whom shall I fear? The Lord is the strength of my life; of whom shall I be afraid?"

He bowed his head and asked the Lord's blessing and protection on the journey ahead. Swinging Barbara to her feet, he placed his arms around her and kissed her lips. With an arm around her he led her to the wagon. Willie had already rolled out his blanket and lay down under the stars. Barbara soon relaxed in Charlie's arms.

After breakfast the next morning, the lone prairie schooner and the quartet of cows picked up the Santa Fe Trail. Wide, with dusty wagon tracks, it meandered toward the West. The slow creak and rumble of the wagon, and low muttering of cows kept a curious rhythm as the little procession crept along. Barbara knew the move could take from nine days to two weeks, and although she was already tired from the tedious rattle of the wagon, she tried to fortify herself with cheery thoughts. The Trail proved easier travel and she knew there would be some diversion from travelers coming from the West, or even stage coaches that sometimes took military personnel to Fort Zarah and Fort Larned. Ahead, the wide, flat plains sloped gradually southwest, and in the distance she saw mere dots that grew slowly larger. It was probably a wagon heading east.

As their schooner pulled to a halt for the nooning, Barbara was happy to stretch her legs while preparing lunch. As she rummaged through their supplies, Willie staked out the cows while Charlie built a fire. The day was quiet, a prairie baking in the stifling summer sun.

The potatoes were sputtering in the skillet when the eastbound wagon reached them. Charlie hurried toward the vehicle as the man in the plaid shirt doffed his grimy felt hat.

"Howdy! Name's Carter. You headin' West?"

"Down to near Pawnee Rock where I've a claim waiting," Charlie said. "Where are you going?"

"Headin' back to Missouri, an' civilization. There ain't nuthin' fer us out West."

"Any dangers?"

The man spat over his horse's back. "Injuns not too cantankerous, with that Fort Larned and Fort Zarah full of so'jers. But it's so blasted lonely. Wife said she'd *walk* back if I didn't take her."

When the wagon creaked on again, Barbara saw the pathetic blur of a sad white face under the starched brim of a faded pink sunbonnet, and her heart gave a sudden lurch. Was the man right? Was it a lonely place? Even worse than Marion Centre when she had come?

"Just some 'go-backers,'" Willie shrugged when they headed around the bend. She was silent during the noon meal, her thoughts in a turmoil. Marion Centre had seemed remote and alone, compared to the graces and gay whirls of Atlanta. Just as she had become used to the little frontier town along the Cottonwood, she had fallen in love with Charlie Warren. And now they were headed for more loneliness.

As Charlie returned from the Carter wagon, he chucked Barbara's chin in his palm. "Anything wrong, my love? You look so forlorn, so . . . so stricken. Sorry already you married me?"

She blinked back the tears. *Dear God, why does it have to be so hard?* she prayed silently. If she had more of Bitsy and Vange's sense of humor she'd find a way to laugh it off.

"Oh, Charlie . . . I . . . I guess I'm a coward, but it scares me to go where there's no one else. I'll follow you wherever you go, but . . ." Sobs tore at her throat.

Charlie pulled her into his arms and kissed her gently, then brushed back the dark curls from her forehead.

"I know, darling. But please believe me, the land is wide open and before long it will be settled. It's a chance in a lifetime to build our ranch. God's in this for us, and I promise you won't be sorry."

Barbara wanted to believe Charlie and it took every ounce of love and faith she possessed to accept his words. When she laid her head against his broad chest, she whispered, "I . . . I'm sorry. I'll be all right. You'll see." Then she pushed him away and went back to the fire.

In the days that followed, Charlie and Willie seemed more concerned for her than usual, she thought, as the wagon moved down the Trail. Willie provided water and firewood when they pulled over to camp. Now and then a stagecoach passed by, for there were frequent stages between Council Grove and Santa Fe in New Mexico. The drivers always stopped and exchanged news.

"Remember, our cabin has two rooms," Willie told Barbara one day when he and Charlie changed about and he handled the team while Charlie wrangled the livestock. "There's a small crick to the north of the claim, and a fresh-dug well near the road. And once we get past Pawnee Rock, we're just about there."

"What's all this about Pawnee Rock?" she asked trying to shade the blazing sun from her eyes by pulling down the brim of her bonnet.

"Well, it's sort of the most dangerous part of the Trail," he said carelessly. "It's a pile of sandstone risin' almost straight up from the Trail. Once we get past it, we'll be fine."

"But why is it dangerous, Willie?" she prodded.

He clucked the team and pressed his lips into a thin line. "Oh, once in a great while Injuns wait on top and when a traveler comes by, they may try a few tricks."

"Like what?" Barbara demanded, her blue eyes wide.

"Oh, you know. Maybe just watchin'. Maybe shoot a few arrows. But that's why Fort Larned and Fort Zarah are there, to guard the Trail. A few Pawnees or Cheyennes, or maybe a Commanche or Kiowa band now and then, manage to squeak past, you know. That's what them soljers is there for. Most Injuns roam west of there. This don't happen often. They tell us scouts like Kit Carson and even General Robert E. Lee have carved their names on the front of that big rock. Don't you worry none, Barbara."

She was silent. Perhaps Willie was right. Maybe she was being unduly alarmed. It was time as a Christian she stopped dwelling on her fears and started looking to the Lord. After having known White Turkey, the Kaw, she had decided not to be afraid of Indians again. White Turkey had once offered 12 ponies for her, and had killed a prairie rattler just before it struck her. Besides, wasn't the Lord with them? Hadn't He promised to guide them?

She had almost talked herself into a cheerful mood when they came into Plains country several days later. The land was flat, and the rolling hills had almost vanished. Buffalo grass, unlike prairie grass, grew flat on the ground instead of in bunches. One thing that drew Barbara's attention was the vast space—the utter, endless stretch of land, barren of trees and streams. She'd thought the land in Eastern Kansas looked drab, but this was even more so. Yet this was what Charlie wanted. He needed space . . . space to let his heart grow, not to mention his dreams. As soon as she saw all the flat, yellowed plain leaning against the sky, she knew Charlie had found his home. She almost looked forward to settling in the little sodhouse, and making a home for her husband and his congenial young brother.

"We're less than a day away from our claim," Charlie told her one evening as they stopped to make camp. "It won't be long now, and we'll be home."

"Willie," he called out, "need help with the cows?"

As Barbara poured the moistened cornmeal into a big skillet

to bake on the fire, she stepped to the wagon for a bit of bacon to crumble on the dough. She remembered how tasty Aggie's cornbread was, with white gravy made from fresh milk.

". . . but you needn't tell her," Barbara overheard Charlie's low voice talking to Willie on the far end of the wagon where the two were washing up.

"She won't hear it from me, Charlie," Willie said. "What exactly did the stage driver tell you yesterday?"

Charlie's words were so low that Barbara strained to hear them.

"Ten teamsters were killed by Sioux. Only Robert McGee survived."

Willie's breath jerked. "That's terrible! But that was—"

Barbara didn't stop to hear more. She hurried back to the fire to tend to the cornbread. A bit of bacon slipped from her hand and hit the glowing red embers. The sizzling sound that it made seemed loud to her ears. She knew they were coming to Pawnee Rock tomorrow.

Her fear of Indians surged through her again. Would the huge, towering rock become the tombstone for their arrow-riddled bodies? Swaying dizzily, she sank to the ground.

CHAPTER 4

*B*arbara slept little that night. Visions of savage Indians screaming with war whoops paraded through her restless mind. Although both Charlie and Willie had assured her the soldiers at the forts along the Trail kept the Indians from attacking stage coaches, the claim was less than two miles off the main road. What was to hinder hungry savages from surging off the beaten path?

She tried to lie quietly in Charlie's arms and took several deep breaths to calm her fears. Yet her heart thudded so hard she could hear its frantic pounding.

"Lord," she prayed for the hundredth time, "please help us make it safely. You know I'm not used to praying and trusting like Charlie and Uncle Daniel's family. Perhaps some day I'll learn. But . . . please, dear Lord, help me to leave it all in Your hands."

Gradually the pounding in her chest eased and she fell into a quiet sleep.

The next morning when she awoke, she heard Charlie snapping twigs and cracking branches as he built the breakfast fire. Willie had been up early, looking after the stock.

Sitting up, she dressed quickly, plaiting her brown hair and forming a tight bun at the nape of her neck. Her blue-checked gingham was grimy from the long ride but there had been no time to wash the basketful of dirty clothes while traveling. She had helped Aunt Prudy enough to know exactly how to wash them by sudsing the clothes in tubs of hot water then rinsing them clear of soap. With a sigh she recalled the time Willie had been so ill with diphtheria and she had stayed those anxious days in the cabin in the glen to nurse him. Boiling Willie's bedclothes and sheets had given her the first taste of taking care of laundry.

Jamming her bonnet on her head, she scrambled down from the wagon and hurried toward the fire which already burned briskly.

"Oh, Charlie," she wailed, "I'm sorry I overslept. But I had such a time falling asleep last night."

"I know, Barbara. You were so tense and tight. I didn't want to disturb you, so I decided to let you sleep this morning."

"You noticed?"

He stirred the fire with a stick. It crackled and sputtered. "Like I said, you were keyed up, I guess, wondering about Pawnee Rock—"

"That wasn't all," she put in, grabbing a skillet and wiping it with a wet rag. "I overheard you and Willie talking about . . . about the teamsters who were killed. That didn't make it any easier."

"No, I guess not." He took her in his arms and kissed her gently, then turned away. "But you didn't hear all of it, did you?"

Barbara didn't answer. She busied herself with fixing breakfast and wasn't sure she wanted to hear more bad news.

Charlie chuckled. "The soldiers who were being pursued, discovered if they threw empty pistols, swords and valises at the Indians, especially the dress uniforms, the savages stopped to try them on and gave up chasing the soldiers!"

"But what about this McGee?" Barbara paused with the cornmeal canister in her hands. "What happened to him?"

"I guess he recovered. All has been peaceful since. As I said before, that's what the forts are there for. To protect the Santa Fe Trail."

Willie sauntered to the wagon and squatted down beside the fire. "What's for breakfast? I'm hungry."

Hurrying with the plates and cups, Barbara soon had the cornbread and bacon ready. She noticed Charlie prayed especially for protection as they neared Pawnee Rock. Somehow Barbara's panic eased, for Charlie's prayers sounded so confident, so full of faith. She felt God was listening.

Along the Trail she could distinguish a blur of buildings to the west.

"That, my dear," Charlie pointed out, "is Fort Zarah. So we're safe."

Before long they were ready to roll. Barbara set her mouth in a grim line, knowing they were nearing the fort. Light-green buffalo grass, covered the stretch of the middle of the Trail. Mere dots were growing larger. In a few moments she saw they were wagons heading East.

As they neared the caravan, the first wagon stopped. A man in a gray shirt hopped from the seat and shuffled toward them.

"Howdy!" He stretched out a rough, horny hand. "Name's Cassidy. You headin' West?"

Charlie had already jumped off to talk. "Yes, I'm Charlie Warren and my wife, Barbara. That's my young brother chasing the cows. You going back East?"

"I figured it was best." He nodded. "My young'uns need a decent spot to grow up. That wild country's no place for a family. But it's great land out there, real perductive."

"How was Pawnee Rock?"

"No problem. Safe as a baby's crib. Don't worry none. It's an in'erestin piece of scenery, though. It was there that Kit Carson, then a scrawny lad, had his first experience with the Pawnees. That's how the rock got its name. Used t' be freighters and trappers hardly escaped a skirmish with either at the Rock or Fort, or Little or Big Coon Creeks. Along the Smoky Hill it's a diff'runt story." He spat out a chaw of tobacco.

"What's along the Smoky Hill?"

"Seems the Cheyennes an' Sioux have been hasslin' the travelers. 'Course, you cain't trust a Pawnee, nor an Apache neither. They really been rampagin' stages."

Charlie shook Cassidy's hand and thanked him. The man hopped back on his wagon and it rumbled down the Trail toward the east.

"See? What did I tell you?" Charlie said, scrambling up beside Barbara and clucking to the team. "Let's just trust the Lord and keep moving."

Before long they saw the pile of reddish sandstone rising abruptly from a fertile stretch of bottom land. The top was almost flat, and it was easy to imagine Comanches or other Plains Indians waiting in ambush when wagon trains approached.

In spite of her determination not to be afraid, Barbara felt herself tense up again.

Willie pulled up on his horse beside the wagon. "Why don't I scout around, just to make sure all's clear?"

"No, Willie!" Barbara cried out. "I won't have you risk your life like that!"

Charlie stroked his chin thoughtfully, then nodded.

"Maybe that's not a bad idea. You're short, and if you'd creep around that big pile of rock and check things out, we'd know if it's safe to pass."

"Charlie!" Barbara snapped. "What are you thinking of? Your only brother—"

"No, Barbara, we've got to do this. Let Willie go. We've prayed and asked the Lord to protect us, and both my brother and I feel easy about it."

Her heart pounding with fear, Barbara lowered her gaze. Where was her faith? She had promised Charlie she would follow him wherever he went, and now she was turning into a shrinking violet again. Finally she nodded.

"All right, Willie," she said in a small voice. "I . . . I guess I need to trust God, too. Go ahead, Willie, but I'll be praying for you every minute."

"We'll wait in that grove of trees," Charlie added. "I'll keep an eye on the stock."

With that he clucked to Pet and Polly and the wagon pulled

toward the fringe of wild plum thicket while Willie scrambled away on foot, skirting the huge rock as he turned slightly north, and crept stealthily toward the rear.

Barbara was quiet, her head bowed in prayer. She heard Charlie's soft whisper of praise and thanksgiving, so sure he was that all was well.

As the two sat on the wagon seat, they grew silent. There was nothing to talk about, only to wait. But the waiting seemed interminable.

Once Charlie looked at her and touched her shoulder. "Willie will be fine," he said huskily. "I'm sure of it."

"I . . . I'm trying to believe it too," she muttered, and drubbed her fingers on her lap.

Half an hour later Willie came running toward them, grinning broadly.

"Everythin's fine. Not a turkey feather anywhere. You should see all them names carved on front of the rock. It was like a history lesson!"

"You mean . . . you stopped and read everything?" Barbara gasped.

"Sure. Names like Gen'ral Lee, Custer, and a bunch of other bigwigs. Let's get goin'. We're almost to our claim. I'm anxious to get home." He scrambled on his horse and kicked her with his heels.

Home. Barbara savored the word with distaste. Then she laughed softly. "I have a pile of laundry to do when we get there, you know."

"First, we'll have to clean the soddy," Charlie said. "It hasn't been lived in for quite a spell."

Slowly the little procession moved back down the Trail. The schooner creaked and rumbled as so many other wagons had done since the historic Trail had opened. The dark shape that loomed ahead seemed to draw nearer, and for a moment Barbara shut her eyes. When she opened them, she saw the scarred, weatherbeaten front, carved with quaint, crude letters. Yes, there were the names of countless men who had made the dangerous and exciting passage along the Santa Fe

Trail while they drove through its shadow. Once they had passed it, Barbara wondered if Willie had scratched his name in the sandstone beside the others.

Charlie turned sharply to the right a mile or two beyond the Trail and followed a dim road northward. The area ahead looked lonely and vast. The sun was already setting and the soft pink turned to brilliant orange as it streaked a few high, cirrus clouds.

Suddenly, Charlie pointed. "There it is—our soddy!"

Barbara squinted. It stood stark and bare against the setting sun, with a ramshackle sod barn behind it. Charlie pulled up and stopped the team beside the large well next to the road, and jumped off. He bounded into the little shanty and pushed open the door, then slammed it roughly before he came back to the wagon.

An overwhelming feeling of loneliness and sadness swept over Barbara. Not another house was in sight anywhere. It was as though they were in the middle of nowhere.

Charlie helped her from the wagon and kissed her lightly. "Before I carry you across the threshold, my darling," he said, "we'll have to clean out the cobwebs and dirt. Let's sleep in the wagon tonight. Tomorrow's another day."

She started to walk toward the door, but he seemed anxious for Barbara not to see the inside of the sodhouse just yet, and she wondered about that. *Was I too hasty in promising to follow him to this lonely place?* she thought. *If only I didn't love him so much . . .*

CHAPTER 5

$\mathcal{T}$he tension of the day before had tired her so much that Barbara's eyelids drooped even before they had finished their meal of cornbread and fried ham. The last of Aggie's dried apple pies was long gone, but Barbara had rummaged among the staples and found several raw Winesaps wrapped in scraps of newspaper. As they munched on their "dessert," the crunch of the apples, the crackle of the fire and an evening prayer of thanks offered by Charlie were the only sounds in the cool, prairie night.

Barbara fell to sleep before Charlie in the wagon that night and it was he who had difficulty sleeping. Barbara was awakened several times from his twisting and turning.

In the morning the early September breeze fanned through the open flaps of the wagon's canvas cover, sweet and dewy. She dressed hurriedly and scrambled to the ground. As usual, Charlie had built the fire and Willie was milking the cows.

Barbara eyed the little sodhouse warily. It looked drab and shabby with its gable roof, and single door facing north. Charlie had boasted that it had a "three-beam" roof, and the walls were made of buffalo grass with a dense root system. This made for durable blocks cut with a sod cutter that sliced strips of sod.

"The well is a good one," Charlie told her as she appeared

for breakfast. "It's off a little on the main road so we'll see movers stopping by for water. It'll take the edge from the loneliness here, because people will come in and visit. At least, that's what Ike Courtney told me."

"Oh, I hope so! Charlie, I had no idea . . . I thought there'd be other settlers."

"There are, darling, but not close by. Believe me, there are people. When the Pike's Peak miners didn't find gold, some came here as this area's first permanent settlers."

The aroma of coffee bubbling in the gray pot distracted him briefly and he picked up the tin cups. "Let's finish our breakfast. After we've eaten, Willie can help you clean the soddy. I've already swept out the cobwebs. Really, it won't be so bad, once we have our things moved in."

The wagon was cramped with the meager furniture and other things they had so carefully packed. Barbara gazed at the scene before her, shimmering in the brightness of the morning sun: the broad, green valley, the sleepy creek drowsing beyond the knoll. It seemed unbelievably peaceful.

When breakfast was over, Willie appeared with two scrub buckets and some rags from the wagon and stopped before her with an exaggerated bow.

"Your scrubbedy-dub, ma'am, at your service. Where do we start?"

She laughed, "Oh, Willie, I haven't even gone inside our palatial home. Let me take a look first."

Charlie had already left to take care of the stock and check the fences. Rather hesitantly, Barbara made her way to the door made of sturdy slabs of pine, and paused in the doorway. There were two rooms, the first one fair-sized. Dust clung to the rafters everywhere, and the four small eight-paned windows were grimy. As she stepped over the threshold, a strange feeling swept over her. The walls appeared to be plastered, but in need of a good whitewash. The floor boards were warped and dirt sifted between the cracks as she walked from one room to the other. There was no ceiling, but wide cottonwood planks were nailed underneath the sod roof. Perhaps with a good scrubbing, it might become livable. There was even a bed frame with a straw tick in the west room.

"Let's get to work, Willie," she called out. "If this is to be our home, we've got to make it fit to live in."

For the next two hours she and Willie tackled the window frames, the panes of grimy glass, and finally the warped floor boards, scrubbing everything with a vengeance. Already she pictured the red checkered curtains on the windows—the ones Willie had packed from the cabin in the glen—and pictures on the walls.

After everything was clean and shining, Willie carted in the bedding—pillows and sheets and quilts which Barbara soon tucked smoothly over the straw tick. Willie would sleep on a bunk in the front room. When Charlie came in he would move the larger pieces of furniture in.

In spite of the sharp, clean smell of the lye soap and hot water, the cabin still looked bleak and shabby. For a moment visions of the large plantation house in Georgia flashed through Barbara's mind. As she thought of the fine old house set in a grove of tall maples and magnolia shrubs, she ached for the busy life of activity with darkies ever puttering, doing the kinds of work she was doing now, and tears sprang to her eyes.

"It's such a *lonely* place, Willie!" she cried, wiping the wet streaks from her dirt-smudged cheeks with one corner of her sleeve.

"But you'll make it home for us, Barbara," he soothed, patting her shoulder. "I know you will. Don't you fret none. Come, let's bring in the chairs and lug in the chest. I think we can manage it. Later, when Charlie comes in we'll cart the topsy stove and table."

They had just dragged her trunk through the door when Barbara thought she heard the clatter of hoofbeats in the yard. Before she had a chance to look, the figure of a big, raw-boned woman filled the doorway, a shapeless, drab, blue dress covering the blurry outline. Her sparse gray hair seemed stretched wire-taut under a huge straw hat.

"Howdy! I'm Mamie Probst—but call me Mame. We live two miles thataway, on t'other side of Turkey Crick. Welcome to the settlement—such as it is."

Barbara's mouth dropped open at the sight of the big, brawny woman who seemed to dominate the room completely.

"Su-prised you, didn't I? Bet you didn't know you had neighbors. There's just me and my husbin' Henry. He's German. We got some young'uns who's all growed up now and gone. This your boy?" She pointed to Willie. "You look mighty young—"

Barbara gulped. She felt overwhelmed by the woman's exuberance. "I . . . I'm Barbara, and this is Willie, my husband Charlie's brother. We . . . We're just getting moved in."

"Sure took a lick of scrubbin' to make it fittin'," Willie offered.

"Looks so-so." Mame nodded. "Now let's get the rest of your stuff moved in."

She grabbed the little trunk and lifted it easily as she carried it into the bedroom. "It b'longs right here at the foot of the bed." Huffing only slightly she bounced back into the kitchen and spied the chest. Shoving it across the bumpy floor, she pushed it to the south wall of the bedroom. "It goes there. Nice to have it where you can get to your duds and stuff."

Barbara stood by helplessly as Mame carried in bags of flour and cornmeal and set them along the south wall of the kitchen. She stacked sacks and cans on the wide window sills.

"What you need here is a shelf or bench to set your staples on," she said with an air of authority.

"Charlie aims to put some shelves over there, beside the stove," Willie told her. "He'll be surprised how easy we're getting things done."

"Where's your table? Your stove? I can bring in the table and unpack dishes." Mame marched through the door, beckoning Willie to follow.

Barbara stared at the broad receding back. Who did Mame Probst think she was, anyhow, taking charge of moving Barbara and Charlie's belongings into the little soddy? She clenched her fists as Willie helped Mame bring in the table. Without a word, the big burly woman pushed it against the east window.

"Here's where it b'longs, so you can ketch the morning sun as you eat breakfast. Be sure to set the topsy stove right under the chimbly. Now, let's get them dishes unpacked. Looks like a handy built in shelf over there."

Mame unwrapped each dish carefully and stacked plates on the shelf while Barbara watched helplessly. After everything was unpacked, Mame sized up the rest of the room.

"Now, you kin hang your curtains and get all your pretties up. I s'pose you got pitchers?"

Barbara caught her breath sharply. "Pitchers? Oh, pictures. Yes, and I know exactly where *I'll* hang them!" She couldn't keep the edge out of her voice.

"Sure, Honey. You just put them where you want. Remember, if you need more help, just call Mame. It's so good to have another woman to neighbor with. I hope you and me'll be good friends." She waddled toward Barbara and gave her a quick hug. "Just don't forget to call on ol' Mame. I better get on home and fix Henry's vittles. Bye now."

With a quick whirl of her blurry figure, she was out the door, swung astride her mule, and clattered away.

Barbara watched her leave, staring a moment at the ungainly departure.

"Well, Willie, what do you make of all that?" she said flippantly.

"Of what, Barbara?"

"Oh," Barbara gestured with her hand, "of that woman who barges in unannounced and takes charge of everthing."

Willie turned away to hid a smile. "Oh, I think she's quite a gal. Reminds me of a rubber ball."

"You remind me of Bitsy! But don't you see, Willie?" Barbara flared. "She took over. She put *my* things where *she* wanted them. She didn't even bother to ask *my* wishes!"

"Well, but you gotta admit, she picked out the best possible places for them. I think she'll make a good neighbor."

"Neighbor!" Barbara spat out, shaking the folded checked curtains and threading one through the string dangling from the east window. "I'd rather be lonely than put up with the likes of that bossy, brassy Mame Probst."

"I'd venture some day you'll be glad to have her around. I think God sent her, like an angel unawares today. Now let's get the rest of them curtains up. When Charlie comes he can get the heavy pieces in, then we're all set. What are you hangin' on the bedroom windows?"

Barbara fretted and stewed the rest of the morning. She couldn't agree with Willie that Mame Probst was God's "angel." What ailed him? Couldn't he see how obstreperous the woman had made herself?

Just then Charlie poked his head into the doorway and gave a low whistle. "Whee! Looks like the two of your worked your heads off. Things are beginning to look nice and homey. How'd you manage to get that trunk and the chest in? Barbara, you're not doing too much, are you?"

She snorted a little. "Your little bride isn't quite as fragile as that. But we had help."

"Help?" He stared at her. "What kind of help?"

"A rubber ball!" Willie laughed. "Name's Mame Probst. She and Henry live on t'other side of Turkey Crick, she said. She came to help. A *big* woman. It didn't take her long to heft things around."

"Where *she* wanted them!" Barbara sniffed. "I didn't have any say-so at all."

She gave the curtains a hard shake as she adjusted the string and evened the shirred panels.

"Well, you can change things to suit yourself," Charlie suggested. "Can't you?"

Barbara didn't answer. Somehow things seemed all right where they were. She'd leave them this way. For now.

After Willie helped Charlie bring in the topsy stove, the cabin took on a more homey look.

"The floor's rough," Barbara said as she brought in the pots and pans, stumbling on the uneven boards. "I know this house has a floor, but it's terribly uneven."

"It's not a grooved flooring, just plain cottonwood planks. But most soddies have dirt floors, so we should be grateful."

"At least the walls are plastered," she conceded.

Charlie looked up from adjusting the stove legs. "Call it plaster, if you wish. But I know how they plaster these soddies."

"What do you mean, Charlie?"

"They use mud and . . . and . . . manure. Then they whitewash—"

"Manure?" Barbara shrieked. "Is that what's on these walls?"

"What'd you use on the walls of your Southern mansions?" he asked cryptically.

"I . . . I don't know. But—"

"See? You can't be sure. I'm sorry darling, but here we do the best with what we have."

I keep forgetting that the old life is behind me, she thought. *And I must accept my new status—that of a frontier wife. God forgive me,* she prayed.

"I'm sorry, Charlie. It's all so strange. I'll have to get used to it."

Charlie came toward her and kissed her on the tip of her nose. "I know. But together, the three of us, we'll get it done. With God's help."

"And with Mame's," Willie added with a grin.

He picked up a picture from the box of things Aunt Prudy had sent along. The words cross-stitched in blue on the white background read:

GOD CARETH FOR YOU.

With a tight smile Barbara held up the sampler. "Where shall we hang it?"

Willie grinned. "Since Mame Probst isn't here to tell us, why not hang it on the east wall, just north of the window?"

CHAPTER 6

$\mathcal{A}$s the days slipped into mid-September, Barbara settled into life in the sodhouse with a round of busy activities. Charlie was building fences with Willie's help when she didn't have work for him.

The soddy was quite comfortable—cool at night and pleasant during the day. The weather was perfect. The grass stretched endlessly for miles toward the ever receding horizon. Wild breezes dipped over the flat plains with a low crooning sound.

At first Barbara was too busy with cleaning and cooking to be lonely. Sometimes when she stepped outside to overturn the milk pails on the fence posts, she stopped to sniff the heath asters that flaunted purple blooms along one side of the lane. Once Charlie brought her a bouquet of rich, yellow goldenrod which she promptly tucked into an empty tin can and set on the kitchen table.

He had stirred up a mixture of lime and water one day and white-washed the inside of the cabin a glistening, sugary white. With the bright cheery curtains on the windows and fresh white walls, Barbara felt the little soddy was beginning to look presentable. On the east wall the cross-stitched frame, "GOD CARETH FOR YOU," was a continual reminder of God's love. Charlie had planted Aunt Prudy's wild rose bush on the east side of the cabin as a final, gentle touch.

To Barbara's delight, an occasional "mover wagon" stopped at the well to water its team, and almost invariably the travelers ambled to the cabin for a brief visit and exchange of news. She tried to keep the cookie tin filled with fresh baked molasses cookies which she offered to her guests, although she knew her cooking skills would never match her Cousin Aggie Moore's.

Willie had a knack of cheering her up when she felt blue. "Remember how your cousins Vange and Bitsy never kneeled under to their bad days?" he reminded her one day. "They always got you thinkin' about somethin' funny."

"Oh, sometimes I got tired of their everlasting fun and good humor," Barbara admitted sheepishly. "But I'd give almost anything now to hear their constant laughing and chatter. Josh used to say they reminded him of a flock of blackbirds in the timber."

"See? That's what I mean."

"But it's so devastatingly lonely here, Willie," she said ruefully. "There's hardly anyone within miles of us, even with the mover wagons stopping by."

"Well, the Probst dugout's just down Turkey Crick a mile or so away. You could always—"

"I'd rather spend my time taking care of the soddy than waste my time dodging her jibes."

Willie picked up the empty wood basket and started toward the door. "Suit yourself. Well, I'd better look for more prairie coal. Wood is scarce, and you gotta have fire to cook."

She watched his thin, 12-year-old figure disappear into the vast grassland. Cooking with buffalo chips was still distasteful to her, but she was learning to adjust. The cracks in the floor always sent up skiffs of dust when anyone walked over it, and sometimes it seemed her broom was in constant motion. A tongue and groove flooring would have helped. Yet there were never any fleas in the house. The little cellar under the kitchen had teemed with bugs—until Willie found a toad which he kept down there. He often played with it and called it "Silas," after Silas Locklin of Marion Centre, the Indian scout.

"Silas the Toad can't track Injuns but he's pretty good about trackin' bugs and fleas under the house," he said when Barbara begged him to get rid of the toad.

Hot, dry days stretched ahead in spite of autumn's calendar. With no garden, their meager supply of food was threatened, and Barbara had to wrack her brains for more appetizing ways to fix cornmeal.

Charlie came in one day with a lighter step than usual. "Barbara, just think what I found in a small patch north of the well. Ike Courtney must've planted some turnips and carrots. If we dig them up we'll have quite a cache of good food stuff until I go after supplies.

He and Willie worked hard all afternoon, scratching up bucket after bucket of the hardy garden vegetables, which Willie carted down to the cellar through the lid that opened from the outside.

One mild Saturday afternoon in early October, two wagons pulled up and stopped to water their teams. Barbara hoped the women would make their way to the door for a brief visit. She hurriedly swept the dirty floor and tidied up the kitchen, straightening the crocheted doily on the clock shelf along the west wall and hanging up the damp tea towels.

She stood in the doorway as Charlie invited the movers into the house. One woman, about age 30, was very obviously pregnant, and with her were two children.

"Come right on in," Barbara called out cheerily. "I'm Barbara Warren. You must be tired. Sit down and rest awhile. Let me fetch you a drink of water. Why don't you take that chair?" She pointed to the only chair near the table. The two children stood politely in the doorway.

The tall, blond woman walked heavily over the threshold and sank into the chair.

"I'm Callie Briggs," she said after she had drained the cup of water Barbara offered her. "These are my Dolly and James. Dolly is eight and James will soon be 11."

"And your husband?" Barbara asked.

Callie shook her head. "Thayne drowned while we were crossin' the Missouri River. We . . . we were travelin' with the Herringtons in the other wagon, so after the accident I continued on with them, since I had no other place to go. Mary Herrington was my sister. But she died giving birth just this side of Independence. The babe was dead, too." She paused and took a deep breath.

"Lucas Herrington has two young'uns names Sarah Lynn and Nelson. Sarah Lynn is 14 so she's some help, but Nelson's only 10. Lucas asked us to travel on with them. We're aimin' to reach Colorado before winter where he hopes to work in the mines. With me bein' in a family way . . ." she paused awkwardly, "I didn't know what else to do. When we get there and my baby is born, maybe I can get a job teachin' school, or somethin'."

"But what if the baby is born before you reach Colorado? That trip's a good six weeks or two months away, isn't it?"

Callie gave a weary nod. "That's just it, Barbara. I'll manage that, unless the baby comes early. With only Lucas to assist me . . ." A flush dyed her face. "It's so embarrassing."

Somehow Barbara sensed a kindred spirit in Callie Briggs. She had to keep them here a bit longer. "Let me fix us all some supper," she said suddenly, hurrying to the pan full of turnips in the corner. "We've got plenty of turnips, and some salt pork. And I can stir up a big pan of cornpone." *I'm glad I learned to fix a tolerable good cornbread these past months*, she told herself.

"But that's too much fuss. We'll manage somehow," Callie said, easing herself out of the chair.

Barbara was already stirring up the cornbread and setting a pot of turnips on to boil.

"Callie, I haven't fixed a company meal since we got here! It'll be a pleasure. Just sit down again."

When Sarah Lynn came in, she took the knife from Barbara's hands and began to scrape carrots. The plump, young teenager seemed to know just what to do.

With the aroma of coffee boiling in the gray pot on the little topsy stove and turnips bubbling in the kettle, the room took on a homey glow, and Barbara found herself humming under her breath.

"Why don't you run out to the wagon for some ham," Callie told Sarah Lynn. "We can't expect these good folks to feed the whole tribe of us so unannounced!"

Before long, supper was on the table. Lucas Herrington strode in to the soddy, a lean giant with a full rusty beard and kind blue eyes. Willie had already ranged the four youngsters to eat on the stone slab before the door, leaving the four adults to the table.

After asking the blessing, Charlie soon shared his dreams about the cattle ranch.

"Take my word for it, Warren," Lucas said, "This isn't very good ranch land. But that's not for me to say. I hope you make it."

"I want to do the right thing," Charlie said. "When Ike Courtney offered to trade claims, I figured it was my chance. There are ranches farther north, they tell me."

Barbara felt at ease with Callie Briggs but wondered how to solve the problem of the oncoming baby with Lucas Herrington as the only other adult in the wagons. Sarah Lynn was a mere teenager.

Just then she heard the familiar clatter of the Probst mule, followed shortly by the slam of the door and Mame's bulky figure in the doorway.

"Oh, I didn't know you was having company," she blustered. "Such a nice brood of young'uns eating out there, too. Where you folks from?"

Barbara and Charlie looked at each other. It wouldn't be easy to explain the Herrington-Briggs situation.

"Well, the Herringtons and Mrs. Briggs stopped to water their teams. We invited them to eat with us," Charlie offered. "If there's anything we can do for you, Mrs. Probst."

Mame teetered on her heels, then cleared her throat. "The reason I came out was to tell you Preacher Shane's stopping over on his circuit tomorrow for a church service. We wondered if you might like to come. We're hoping the Frosts over t' Fort Larned will join us."

"Divine services? Why of course." Charlie said heartily. "Where will the service be held?"

"Our dugout ain't big, but we can squeeze together. Now y'all be sure and come." Mame started for the door, then turned around. "Where's Miz Herrington? She ain't along?"

Barbara lowered her head. "She died in childbirth several weeks ago. She was Callie Briggs' sister. The Briggs and Herringtons were traveling together when Callie's husband lost his life so—"

Mame raised one eyebrow in a sharp arch. "So? And Miz Briggs in a family way, too! Tch-tch." She shook her head sagely.

Barbara felt her dander rise. "What else could they do? They were on their way to Colorado, hoping to reach it before bad weather sets in."

"Well now, why don't Mr. Herrington and Miz Briggs get hitched? Thataway she'll have a husbin' and he kin deliver the young'un when it comes. It's that simple."

With a gasp, Barbara jumped to her feet. Mame had opened her mouth in her own brash way and stuck her foot in it again.

"Mame, that's their business, I should think!" she flared. "Not ours, not yours."

Mame shifted her weight from one leg to the other. "But there ain't a thing wrong with such an answer to this problem, is there? Now be sure all of you come to our dugout at two o'clock tomorrow afternoon. Brother Shane will be extra happy for a nice congregation. Bring along some vittles and we'll eat after the preaching." Without a backward glance she bounced from the cabin and clattered away on her mule.

The room was quiet, and the flush still dyed Barbara's face. *The nerve! The gall of that woman to suggest something like that!*

Charlie got up from the table and picked up his straw hat. "Time to take care of the chores and get the cows milked," he said in an awkward silence.

Lucas Herrington jumped up, too. "Let me help, Charlie. I need to graze our teams anyway." Turning to Callie, he said, "Would you like to stay and go to the preaching tomorrow? It's be so long since we've heard a good gospel message. I know we need to get on to Denver, but . . ."

Callie nodded quietly, then began to gather up the plates. "Yes, you're right. We need God's leading in everything about this journey. The children haven't heard good preachin' in weeks."

As the two men left the soddy, Callie turned troubled eyes on Barbara. "Oh, I don't know what to do about that woman's idea . . . about me marryin' Lucas. It's ridiculous. Still, what do you think, Barbara?"

Barbara drew her breath sharply. The idea was preposterous, of course. Yet it was a solution. Somehow she knew the matter wouldn't be dropped lightly.

CHAPTER 7

$\mathcal{A}$s Barbara got out the dishpan and washed the dirty plates and cups, Callie picked up the dish towel and began to dry them. She looked around the cabin and beamed.

"You've got a nice place, Barbara. I'll never forget how kind you were to put us up, not even knowin' who we was."

"You've no idea how much it means to have you," Barbara said, plunging flatware into the soapy water. "I . . . I wasn't always this way. I grew up in Georgia, the daughter of a plantation owner. When the war came we lost everything. And then my father was killed. Mother died not long after. I was forced to leave my safe, happy life and move to Kansas to live with my Uncle Daniel Moore and his family in a two-roomed log cabin near Marion Centre. Can you imagine what a jolt it was, to move from a gracious house to a squatty log cabin? But they were so good, and I didn't appreciate all they did for me, until Matthew, my betrothed, was killed in battle. I had nowhere to turn, except to the Lord.

"When it was almost too late, I discovered I loved Charlie, and we were married in August just a few weeks ago. This is where he wanted to go. But it hasn't been easy. I . . . I'll admit I was spoiled, used to being waited on by a crew of darkies. And now living in this crude soddy . . ." She shook her head. "Life has changed so drastically for me. And it's been so . . .

so lonesome here." Her lustrous blue eyes filled with tears.

"God won't fail you, Barbara. You'll make it. But what am I to do? Is that Probst woman right? Should I marry Lucas?"

Barbara put the dishes on the shelf on the south side of the room before answering. "What I say won't matter. It's what you know is right, Callie. It took me a long time to realize Charlie was right for me. Almost too long."

"Lucas is a good man, a kind, generous God-fearing man, even though he's 10 years older. We've known each other for a long time, ever since he married my older sister, Mary. But after Thayne was killed . . ." She paused, her voice thick with tears.

"Perhaps it would be best all around, Callie," Barbara said gently. "You'd be taken care of, I'm sure."

"Yes, I know. He . . . it would be up to him to . . . to ask me, though." She hung up the dish towel over the back of the one good chair, and the two women walked to the bedroom window to watch the sunset. Already the sky was splashed with reds and oranges that slowly faded into pale pink and mauve before the horizon began to darken.

"Barbara?" Charlie called from the kitchen. "Are you here?"

She took Callie's arm and the two women walked into the room where Charlie and Lucas waited. Outside they heard the shouts and laughter of the children as they romped in the yard. Barbara was glad for Willie's sake that he could join the fun of other young folks again. He'd been away from Marion Centre for two months now.

Lucas came slowly toward Callie and took her hands in his. "Charlie and I have been talking, Callie, . . . about what Mrs. Probst said awhile ago . . . about you and me getting married. I realize Thayne hasn't been gone long, nor has Mary. But you need me, we need each other. And I know what a fine woman you are. Would, would you be willing to marry me tomorrow while the preacher is here? I know it doesn't give you much time to think about it. But this way I could take proper care of you and your children. I'll never ask you to forget Thayne. But we could share our lives and raise our children with God's help."

Callie looked down at her heavy body for a moment. Then she nodded.

"Yes, Lucas. If you are sure and if the children agree. They must be a part of this decision."

"Yes, of course, Callie."

"I'll call them right away," Barbara said, moving swiftly toward the door. "We'll all attend church tomorrow together. Won't that be good?"

With a bustle and a jumble of chatter and laughter, the four cousins scrambled into the kitchen and lined up politely along the north wall.

"Your parents have something to say to you," Barbara said, and nodded to Lucas, who promptly explained the situation to the two sets of children. Willie stood in the background, a wide grin on his freckled face.

"We'd all be together as before, but instead of merely being cousins, you'd be brothers and sisters. But we want to be sure how you feel."

James and Dolly nudged each other, and Nelson turned to Sarah Lynn. After a whispered consultation, Sara Lynn moved shyly toward Callie and took her hand.

"It'll be strange calling you Ma instead of Aunt Callie, but we . . . we all think it's a fine idea." The other three agreed noisily.

For a minute everyone stood silent as the impact of the momentous decision hit them. Then the noise and clamor began until Barbara clapped her hands for attention.

"Look—we have a busy day tomorrow, if we're to plan a wedding and go to church. I advise you to scoot to bed early—all of you!"

"Don't forget about the 'vittles' we're to bring along," Willie piped up. "What we need is a couple of prairie chickens. I remember how good Aggie Moore's always was."

Lucas promptly took his brood to his wagon to sleep while Callie bedded down in her own with Dolly and James.

For a long time that night, Barbara lay awake staring out the little window at the yellow cowslip prairie moon that already tiptoed high into the black heavens. It was quiet, with only the creaky fiddling of crickets and other insects in the brush. She had so much to think about: Willie and Sarah Lynn must look for a smattering of windflowers that still dotted the stretches of brown grass.

Callie's too large to wear my old green bombazine, she thought. *But she needs a crown of blossoms for her hair.* Lying tense and awake beside Charlie, she tried not to stir. Suddenly he whispered against her ear.

"You're not asleep, Barbara, and I know you're thinking about a lot of things. What can I do to help whip up the wedding in a hurry?"

Barbara sighed. "Oh, Charlie, it's the food I'm worried about. Willie's right. We need some meat. We're running low on supplies, and we're bringing six guests to the Probst dugout! How will we ever feed them all?"

"As soon as it's daylight and the chores are done, I'll take my gun and go hunting. I haven't seen any squirrels around, or else you could fix a squirrel casserole."

"Charlie Warren, that was Mindy Harris' specialty!" Barbara squealed. "Bitsy used to say Mindy's soap tasted better than her food."

"I know you threw together our wedding in a hurry, and you'll do fine now. And we'll come up with enough food. Don't worry. Better get some sleep now, darling. You'll be worn to a rag before morning if you don't get some rest."

With a contented sigh she snuggled against Charlie's shoulders and closed her eyes. When she opened them it was morning. Charlie's side of the bed was empty.

Barbara dressed hurriedly and fixed platters of flapjacks with molasses for breakfast while Charlie and Willie looked after the chores. After the meal the little sodhouse bustled as Callie washed the girls' hair and plaited them into fat braids.

After stirring up a loaf cake with the last of her flour, using two of her precious hoard of hen's eggs, Barbara took Sarah Lynn aside.

"Could you help Willie look for flowers for Callie? I know

it's autumn and most everything's bloomed out, but it's the least we can do for the bride."

Sarah Lynn's eyes danced. "I'll be most happy to help. I'm so glad we'll all be one family, Mrs. Warren. And when the new baby comes—"

"You'll make a fine nurse, Sarah Lynn," Barbara said, checking her supply of bread. There were still two loaves left from her last baking.

While Callie dug out Dolly's prettiest blue-dotted Swiss from her trunk, Barbara heated the flat irons on the topsy stove. She still hadn't mastered the art of ironing to her satisfaction, but everyone must look their best on this very special day. And if Barbara could help it, this day would be special for Callie and Lucas and their children.

At 10 o'clock Charlie strode into the kitchen and tossed two jackrabbits on the table. "Think that'll help out? I'm lucky to have shot them as quick as I did. Here, let me pack the basket while you fry them."

Barbara's face grew pink and flushed from bending over the stove, and her hair escaped from its bun and feathered damply around her forehead. She mustn't forget to pack dishes for them all. Finally she changed into her faded pink delaine and combed her blowsy hair.

After what seemed like hours, the procession of three wagons started for the Probst dugout, creaking over the rutted trail that crawled along the shallow creek. Willie knew exactly where to cross the stream. The prairies stretched firm and wide to the rim of the sky in the bright October afternoon.

Ahead lay the dugout where the ravine was shallow. The builder had simply scooped a hole with a natural roof back into the banks of the the stream, some 14 feet wide, and had fashioned a front, laying up sod blocks several feet high. A single ridge pole held up the roof, and only the stove pipe protruded from its grassy top.

Already one or two other teams were tied to the hitching post. Barbara wondered who else had crossed the flat prairies to hear the preacher.

Mame stood beaming in the doorway while Henry helped unharness the teams. As the small congregation trooped into the crowded dugout's low room, Barbara blinked her eyes in the dimness. In spite of the hard-packed dirt floor the little house seemed tidy and neat.

Shooing her guests onto the seats made of logs placed on kegs, Mame seemed to dominate the room with her bulky presence. She had pulled on a rusty black dress that reminded Barbara strangely of Aunt Prudy's "Sunday best," and her eyes misted a little, remembering.

Soon Henry stomped in, followed by a smallish, balding man in a gray coat with mismatched gray trousers, carrying a tattered Bible.

"Welcome here," Henry boomed heartily in his German accent. "So happy Preacher Shane could come here today to hold a service and do a vedding. Now, shall we sing?"

Pitching the opening, he led out too high, and the dugout rang with "Showers of Blessing." Charlie's deep bass carried the low notes with gusto. Barbara smiled, knowing how her cousin Bitsy would say he sounded just like a bullfrog along the Cottonwood. I never knew Charlie sang like that, Barbara mused.

The Frosts from Fort Larned sat behind them. Mrs. Frost was a pale, thin little scrap of a woman with a straggle of red hair wound into a tight knot on top of her head. Captain Frost looked dignified and stern in his blue army uniform. She knew he was one of the officers from the fort. There were three bouncy, wriggling blond children.

After a lengthy prayer, the preacher moved to the front and opened the shabby Bible. He reminded Barbara vaguely of Elder Buck, but without the elder's obvious finesse, or his squeaky boots.

"I'm reading from Matthew 11. 'For where two or three are gathered in My name, I am in the midst of them.' Beloved, we are gathered here to worship our Lord Jesus. This is not some vast cathedral or shrine, but He has promised to be with us as long as we're assembled together. He don't confine His presence to a formal church, for He hath said, 'Lo, I am with you always.' His love follows us wherever we go, and His grace can save us wherever we are."

The message was simple and direct, but it was like a drink in a thirsty land. A tear slid down Barbara's cheek as she remembered that day after Baby Sammie had died and she had seen his mother Rosie's radiant face. It had helped Barbara decide to let God take charge of her life. She had surrendered her stubborn will to Him, and peace as she had never known before had flooded her heart.

"Dear Lord," she whispered under her breath, "Thank You for loving me so much! Help me never to doubt Your unconditional love."

At the close of the service Preacher Shane asked Lucas and Callie to step forward, and he conducted the brief wedding ceremony. Callie's crown of goldenrod and spears of yellow sorrel drooped low on her forehead, but to Barbara, Callie was a beautiful bride—determined, brave and faithful, in spite of her ballooning waistline. She was glad the baby would have a loving father and a host of siblings to welcome it. She hoped she had done the right thing in encouraging Callie to marry Lucas.

After the service Mame hurried outside to the shade of the south side of the dugout and spread a green-checked cloth on the ground, and began to carry out pots of jellied pig's feet, tureens of dried boiled corn, augmented by Barbara's two stewed rabbits. The cake had turned out better than she'd expected, although it sagged a little in the middle. At least Callie and Lucas could boast of a wedding cake.

It was almost a festive occasion, and Barbara reveled in the happy laughter and heartfelt congratulations that swirled over the wedded pair. She was glad she had played a small part in making this special time for Callie and Lucas Herrington. Willie had seemed alive and happy in Nelson and James' company.

Callie gave Barbara a warm hug. "Thanks for makin' this such a special day for us!" she cried.

"Now, ain't you glad I se'jested this hitch?" Mame Probst stood at Barbara's elbow. "Looks like my plans worked out fine. And looks like everyone's enjoyin' the vittles."

Barbara bristled a little. In spite of everything, she found it hard to agree that Mame's idea had been a good one—when she deserved some credit herself.

CHAPTER 8

$\mathcal{B}$arbara felt a deep sense of loss when Callie and Lucas and the children left early on Monday. The morning was chilly and a V-shape of geese winged in formation as they honked their way south.

Knowing the Herringtons hoped to reach Denver before the first snowfall, Barbara worried about Callie's baby that was due in barely two months. Callie had promised to write as soon as they reached their destination, but Barbara knew the trip would be tiring under any circumstances.

Charlie had sold some sheep wool from shearing his flocks weeks before the flood took them. He'd saved the money to buy the needed supplies for winter. In early November he planned a trip to Ellsworth to buy lumber and food for the long months ahead. Although the mornings were cool, the days were mild with warm, dry sunshine.

"We must winterize the soddy before cold weather sets in. Everything's peaceful, and I'm sure you and Willie will be fine until I get back. I should be gone only a few days."

"A few days!" Barbara echoed. "But Charlie—"

"It's time to go *now*. We must brace the walls against the winter winds, even though the soddy's quite snug," he said. "And the chicken coop is small. I want to make it safe from thieves and coyotes. You know I don't like to leave you and

51

Willie, but I'll be back as soon as I can. Maybe Henry Probst could look in on you now and then, and Fort Larned's nearby."

A feeling of despair welled over Barbara as she watched his wagon ride out of sight. But she realized that if he didn't go soon, the mild days for working outdoors would be over.

Willie eyed the woodshed sharply after he came in from the barnyard. "Barbara, the pile of chips is gettin' mighty low. I promised Charlie I'd pick up a bunch in the little cart he made for haulin' water to the stock. One of these days it'll get cold and we'll need plenty to feed the topsy."

"Are there any buffalo chips left?"

"We've been pickin' them up pretty fast, but I know there are far more farther south. Besides, our own stock has added some by now."

Barbara pressed her lips together firmly. She detested this "prairie coal" but it had its uses. "Willie, can I help?" she added suddenly. "I don't like to stay in the house alone. If I help you lug them home, we'll soon have a good-sized pile, and I'll be less lonely that way."

"Well," he said with a wide grin spreading over his freckles, "I never dreamed you'd help me pick up anything as . . . as nasty as 'prairie coal'!"

"I'm not saying I'll like it," she flared. "But if it means you'll be done sooner, I guess I can do it. I'm baking bread, but while the dough is rising, I'll give you a hand."

A few minutes later, Barbara and Willie pushed the small hand cart over the south prairie, loading up chips. As much as Barbara hated the job, it took her away from the lonely soddy.

Before long they had filled the cart with the fuel which Willie piled in the small shed Charlie had built on the south side of the house. At least they'd have plenty for awhile.

The air had warmed again and she unbuttoned her wrap. When she started toward the house, she noticed a wagon stopping by the well at the end of the lane. It looked decrepit and rickety. She remembered the delightful time she'd had with Callie and Lucas and their brood only two weeks ago, and she brightened at the sight of the thin, slatternly woman in a drab brown dress who had let herself from the wagon and headed toward the house.

Barbara smoothed her wrinkled, dusty skirt as she hurried to the house. The bread dough was rising in the pans and would be ready for the oven about now. Before she reached the door she called out to the woman. Company always eased her loneliness.

"Welcome to our home! Would you like to come in and rest while your husband waters the team?" she said eagerly.

The woman ambled up to Barbara and stuck out a sallow hand. "I'm Liz Harnish and that-there's Clem. We're much 'bliged, ma'am."

"And I'm Barbara Warren. Come on in." She opened the door and beckoned Liz inside.

She stirred the fire, shoved the two loaves of bread into the topsy's tiny oven, and set the gray enameled coffee pot on the front burner. Soon the aroma of bubbling coffee permeated the room.

"Ummm," Liz sniffed. "Somethin' sure smells good."

"I bake bread every other day," Barbara said with a little laugh. "You should see my family eat. Here, take that chair. I'll have coffee ready in a minute."

"Don't mind if I do."

Liz flopped into the one good chair and took off her faded brown bonnet. Her stringy gray hair tumbled from a wispy bun. She watched Barbara silently for about 10 minutes.

"Where are you folks headed?" Barbara asked finally, pouring two steaming cups of coffee.

"We . . . we're headin' west. Don't rightly know just where."

"But surely you have an idea."

Liz looked around the room with a satisfied smirk as she sipped coffee noisily and watched as Barbara opened the oven door to check the bread. It was starting to brown. Chips did make a good fire, Barbara had to admit.

"I suppose your wagon is warm enough? The wind has turned chilly at night," Barbara ventured to break the awkward silence.

"Oh, we got blankets. Even a few buffler robes."

"I'd think you'd need them. You can never out-guess Kansas weather, you know." As the aroma of bread baking filled the kitchen, she refilled the coffee cups.

"Oh, we manage." Liz paused, then sniffed again. "That bread bakin' shore smells good."

Barbara took out the two loaves shortly and placed them on a rack on the table to cool. Then she took a small crock of butter from the shelf. With a few deft strokes she sliced through the hot bread and spread a slab with a generous layer of butter that oozed in yellow rivers down the crusty sides.

Liz reached for a slice greedily and stuffed half a slice into her mouth at once. "Say, Barb'ra, this is . . . real good!" she muttered. Without another word she got up and waddled out the door.

Barbara smiled. She always appreciated travelers who visited as they stopped by for water, but this woman wasn't overly talkative.

The Harnish wagon was still parked beside the lane after the noon meal. Barbara had barely cleared the table when Liz was at the door again.

"Clem wants to know if we could stay here with the wagon for the night. With the well so handy and all—"

"Why," Barbara hesitated only a second. "I'm sure Charlie wouldn't mind. You might as well park here as some other place."

As Liz started for the door, Willie slammed into the kitchen carrying the carcass of a jack rabbit. "Look what I got, Barbara! The trap I made really works good. I skun it so all you need is to flour and fry it for supper."

"Fine. It'll be very tasty with the fresh bread." She got out a pan and poured cold water over the rabbit.

"I'll haul another load of chips while I'm out," he said, and hurried away. Liz was gone when Barbara turned around to talk to her guest.

The afternoon seemed to fly by. After getting out the pile of mending, she patched Charlie's extra pair of trousers that had sprung a hole on one knee. Lucky Aggie had shown her how to sew neat patches, although Barbara's weren't anything like Aggie's.

At a sound by the door, Barbara looked up. It was Liz again.

"Wonder if we could borry some eggs," she said. "We noticed the hens."

"Of course," Barbara said, laying aside her mending. "I'll see if Willie's back from hauling chips, and send him for some fresh ones from the nests." She hurried to the door and called, "Willie, would you please get a couple of fresh eggs for the Harnishes? They need some for their supper."

"My, but it must be nice to have so much," Liz said, an interested gleam in her faded eyes. "Chickens, cows and even a rabbit trap. Did you boy ketch a mess?"

"Just enough for our supper," Barbara said as Willie came back in with the eggs. "Here are two fresh ones for you, Liz."

Liz grabbed the eggs, one in each hand, and pattered across the threshold, then ambled to the wagon without a word of thanks.

"How do you s'pose she expects to return the eggs she 'borried,' Barbara?" Willie asked, his eyes twinkling.

"Oh, Willie," Barbara said. "I'm so lonely. Can't you see? It's good to have people around. Remember when the Lucas Herrington tribe stopped here? It was so good to have visitors!"

"Well, they were people, Barbara. Not pests."

"Pests?" Barbara looked puzzled. She cut the rabbit into pieces for frying.

"Prairie plagues. Pests. Grasshoppers. Like Pharaoh in Egypt."

"The Harnishes are weary travelers, Willie," Barbara said testily, getting out the skillet. "The Bible says to be hospitable to strangers. They asked if they could stay over and rest, and I'm sure they'll leave in the morning. It's the least we can do—to let them stay overnight."

Willie shrugged his shoulders and humped away. Barbara watched him go. Now what was he implying? That the Harnishes were taking undue advantage of the hospitality? *They must be in need*, she thought, *even if Liz doesn't talk much*. She wished Charlie were home. He'd know how to explain to Willie.

The evening was chilly, and Barbara and Willie played checkers near the fire until bedtime.

The next day the Harnishes were still there at mid-morning. Liz was at the door just as Barbara took a pan full of molasses cookies from the oven.

"Ummm," Liz sniffed. "Shore smells good. I wondered, could we borry a bit of bacon? And a tater or two? We've got real low on supplies."

"Well," Barbara hesitated. Surely the Harnishes would leave soon. "I . . . I guess so. My husband is stocking up with supplies right now. They must last all winter, you know."

Liz watched in silence as Barbara wrapped a chunk of bacon in a clean rag and picked up two potatoes from the pail behind the stove.

"Here. I hope you'll enjoy your meal," she said.

The woman hesitated, her gaze shifting to the warm cookies on the table. "Them shore smells good. Bet they's molasses too."

"Yes, they are. I'm still learning how to cook," Barbara said awkwardly as she picked up a handful of cookies. Liz pawed them greedily.

"I shore do thank you, Barb'ra. 'Course, I didn't mean for you to give me some. But thanks all the same." She swung around and waddled out the cabin.

Willie came in with a bucket of fresh eggs. "What did Liz 'borry' this time?"

Barbara whirled on him. "Willie, they'll leave soon. Don't be so unkind, please!"

"Sure. Maybe they'll leave, but not 'til they've borried eveythin' we own."

He was out of the house before Barbara could reply.

She went to the east window and looked out. The wagon was still parked by the well. Was Willie right? Were the Harnishes "pests," borrowing or conning all they could get their hands on? True, Liz had little to say, and there seemed to be small warmth in her.

Barbara Warren, where's your Christian spirit? she chided herself severely. What if she hadn't given the Herringtons-Briggs party any consideration? They'd have missed out on a wonderful time together. But the Harnishes frankly puzzled her.

The interminable day wheeled slowly to a close. She took the milk pail from beside the door and went to look for Willie. He'd kept to himself, and had hardly been in all afternoon. It was time he milked the cows.

The sun had left its smoldering fire in the west, its embers flaring briefly before fading to gray ashes. Willie had already brought the cows into the corral. Only Bess was giving milk now, and as he sat down to milk, Barbara leaned over the fence to watch him and offered her help. After he handed the milk pail to her, she started toward the soddy.

Liz was waiting for her at the door. "You wouldn't have a drop or so of milk to spare, would you? 'Course, I don't want to run you short."

Barbara slammed the pail down a trifle abruptly. "Bess isn't giving as much as she should, and the other cows are dry. But, I guess we could spare a little."

As she went into the kitchen, Liz followed her in, leaving the door open. Barbara got a clean cloth and strained a quart of the warm, foamy milk into the little tin pail Liz held out to her. Liz walked around the kitchen, fingering the curtains, and then the amber dish on the clock shelf which Grandma Griffith had given her and Charlie as a wedding gift. The gust of cold air that blew through the open door seemed to chill Barbara and she went to shut it.

"You shore have purty things, Barbara," Liz said, touching the fluted edges. Barbara watched her uneasily.

Lighting the candle, Barbara set it on the table. Its flickering light flung eerie shadows in the dark corners and through the windows into the deepening twilight.

Suddenly she wished Liz would leave. The woman gave her

an eerie feeling. Would she ask for the amber dish next?

"When . . . will you be leaving?" Barbara said finally.

Liz whirled around. "Clem ain't said."

"Perhaps you better move along while the weather's holding out."

"Guess so," Liz shrugged.

After Liz left with the milk, Barbara began to prepare supper. Willie burst through the door and tossed his wraps on the floor. She was about to tell him to hang them up when he turned troubled eyes toward her.

"Barbara, when's Charlie comin' home? I sure wish he was here now."

"So do I." She turned from the stove where she was turning the bacon. He stared at her, his eyes deep and piercing.

"I guess you're puzzled about those folks. They sure make me feel creepy."

She sighed. "But what can we do to make them leave? We don't want to appear unkind."

"Ask yourself, 'What would Mame Probst do in this situation?' "

"I don't know and I don't care!" Barbara flared. "What does Mame have to do with it? I just wish they'd leave!"

Before she went to bed that night she latched the kitchen door securely. She hoped the Harnishes didn't have their eyes on the few hens in the coop. She tossed restlessly all night, sitting up at every swish of wind that gusted under the eaves. Charlie would be home by the next evening she was sure.

Please keep us safe from these weird visitors, she prayed over and over. I've got to do something. But what? Finally she drifted into an uneasy sleep.

In the morning she pulled on her cape and bonnet and hurried out to the well for fresh water. The Harnish wagon was still there. It was quiet. She heard their bony horses whinny in the clump of wild plum bushes. Then she saw Liz Harnish hop from the rear of the wagon, seemingly to watch Barbara warily. *Like a cat with a mouse,* Barbara thought. *She'll be at the door.*

When Barbara came back to the house, Willie was stirring from under the covers. Suddenly Barbara had an idea. Slamming down the pail of water she barreled toward him.

"You stay in bed!" she hissed, and gave him a cuff that made him howl. "I just want you to stay there, hear?" she yelled. "Oh, forgive me Willie!" she breathed. Just then the suspected knock sounded on the kitchen door. Liz stood in the doorway with the queer, begging look in her eyes. The moment had come.

"Wonder if we could borry . . . what's the boy screechin' like that fer?" she swept into the kitchen, suddenly dominating the scene. Willie whimpered in the background and Barbara was afraid to look at him.

Swallowing hard she stared coolly at Liz Harnish. Then she leaned toward the woman and whispered, "He's been quite poorly, Liz. What if it's . . . cholera?"

"Chol . . . cholera!" Liz' jaw sagged. With a sudden whirl, she paused a few seconds and headed for the door like a deflated balloon. The slam echoed dully through the house long after she had fled. The only sounds were Willie's whimpering sobs.

Barbara turned to him and threw her arms around him.

"Oh, Willie, Willie, I'm so sorry! Please forgive me. I just had to do *something*!"

He choked back his tears and a feeble grin crept over his freckles. "It's all right, Barbara. But for a minute I was scared that this lonely place had got you, and you'd really gone daft!"

"I guess, I . . . was." She wiped the tears from her eyes and laid a gentle hand on his shoulder. "Well, you just stay in bed while I fix you a heaping plate of flapjacks. You deserve a special breakfast after the horrid way I acted."

As she vigorously beat eggs into a bowl and added flour and milk, Willie called her name softly.

"Listen!" he said in a strangely lilting voice.

Barbara paused. She heard the distinct creak of the Harnish wagon as it moved down the lane.

Leaving her pancakes for a minute, Barbara went to the

door and opened it a crack. Sure enough, the decrepit old wagon and the bony team were lumbering down the trail.

Willie, crouching behind her, howled with laughter. After he caught his breath he muttered, "You know something, Barbara? You sounded just like Mame Probst just then—bossy and sassy!"

Barbara felt a flare of anger at this flippant words. How dared Willie compare her with the obstreperous Mame? Then the humor of the situation struck her and she grabbed him and hugged him tightly. "Oh, Willie! Willie!"

"Ain't you scared of cholery?" he teased.

"For once, I'm not scared of *anything*!"

Then a thought struck her. I never once told Liz Harnish about the Lord. What if the Harnishes don't know our loving Savior? She gazed gratefully around the room. It was true. She had so much.

Suddenly she noticed a bare spot on the east wall. The cross-stitched verse, "GOD CARETH FOR YOU," was gone. Undoubtedly Liz had snatched it before she slammed from the kitchen.

"Dear Lord," Barbara prayed weakly, "Let that verse speak to them, somehow."

CHAPTER 9

$\mathcal{T}$he gray days of November slunk past like giant timber wolves on the prowl. Charlie had chinked the sod walls with Willie's help and nailed strong pine planks to the rafters throughout the cabin with the heady scent of sawdust clinging in the air. It provided a sturdy ceiling to trap the warmth of the topsy stove in the two tiny rooms.

The days seem like the weather—uninteresting, gray, monotonous, Barbara thought as she pushed her way inside, carrying a pail of water. She set down the pail and shed her wrap.

"Wonder how Lucas and Callie are making out," Charlie mumbled, his mouth full of nails. He had nailed the last plank on the ceiling and stood back to survey his work.

"Wasn't Lucas goin' to prospect for gold?" Willie asked, sweeping the siftings of sawdust from the wide board floor.

"According to Ed Manson out at Ellsworth, gold is just thick around Denver. Wouldn't Callie look classy in earrings made of gold ore?" Charlie joshed.

Barbara snorted. "You sound just like Bitsy. Can you imagine it? Callie strolling down Denver streets, chunks of gold dangling from her ears!"

"Well, they'd have to travel some to reach Denver before the first snow flies. . . . And the passes are prob'bly snow-packed by now," Willie added. "Nelson told me he hoped they'd move some place with a school."

"Willie," Barbara jerked off her bright wool cap, "that reminds me. We've neglected your education since we moved here. As soon as Charlie can do without your help outdoors, we'll open the books again."

"Aw, Barbara, do I have to? There ain't a school around here for miles. You know that!" he grimaced.

"Don't forget I helped Rebecca Shreve at Marion Centre," she chirked. "It'll make the dreary days go faster and you'll get some 'larnin' ' besides."

"Great idea." Charlie placed his right arm gently around Barbara's shoulders. "The jobs between chores I can handle myself. Tomorrow you dig out the school stuff from the trunk, because Warren School will officially open with the first gong of Bo's sheep bell."

"How'd you manage to save the bell from the bellwether before the flood swept from the banks of the Cottonwood, Charlie?" Barbara prodded.

"Believe it or not, Barbara, that morning I took off the bell because the strap was worn and I wanted to replace it with a fresh thong of leather. I stashed it away somewhere among my tools. Maybe it's in the shed."

"So what other excuse can you think of?" Barbara looked pointedly at Willie.

He screwed up his nose. "None, I guess. Just don't make me draw turkeys and Injuns for Thanksgivin'. I'm too big for that!"

Barbara glanced at Charlie. "That reminds me. How *will* we celebrate Thanksgiving in the middle of nowhere?"

"You mean, if we don't have anything to be thankful for? But we do have lots to be thankful for!"

"Like what?" Her voice was a trifle irritable. "This is the loneliest place this side of Siberia. You can't deny that. And with no family nearby—"

"I'll ketch another jackrabbit and you can stuff it," Willie joshed hanging up the broom. "You could whip up a sweet tater pie or two, couldn't you, Barbara?"

She sighed. "Jackrabbit for Thanksgiving dinner? How utterly preposterous! Well, I'm not Aggie, you know, that I can cook a meal from a handful of bacon drippings and some rye. But, I'll try the sweet potato pie."

"How's the ceiling look?" Charlie asked, picking up his tools and wiping his dirty hands on his trousers.

"It's no plantation home, but it'll do." Barbara didn't mean to sound harsh, but she wasn't in a very gallant mood that morning.

The next several days the cabin seemed to sputter with warmth as the quiet murmur of a school room dominated the little cabin. Willie's lessons were going well when he applied himself, and Barbara called him her "prize pupil."

"Yeh, the only pupil, ya mean!" he snapped.

With parsing, spelling, diagramming, fractions and reading *Ivanhoe*, the days passed.

The day before Thanksgiving the weather turned suddenly cold. A drizzle whipped across the plains, dampening the dry, gray prairie grasses to a dull brown.

Charlie stomped in with a grouse he had shot along the fence row, and Barbara knew their Thanksgiving dinner would be bountiful after all. She was sure he had hunted for hours to provide more than one skinny jackrabbit. She struggled with the yams sweetened with honey, and turned out two tasty-looking pies. If ever she missed Uncle Daniel's family, it was probably most at mealtime when Aggie usually outdid herself in the kitchen. Barbara chided herself for her ungratefulness and ticked off three things for which to be thankful: Charlie, Willie and the Lord. That was about all she could think of right now.

December stole in as bleak and gray as November had tiptoed out. Barbara tried to teach Willie the fundamentals of learning in a fuzzy whirl of explaining fractions as she boiled chunks of venison for onion and potato stew. In the back of her mind she thought about Christmas and what a hollow mockery the season of peace and goodwill toward men would be here in western Kansas with so few people. She couldn't get over her feeling of utter dejection.

Charlie had emptied out his wallet on the kitchen table one night before they went to bed. Willie, exhausted after a bout with the sniffles and wrestling with decimals, had already fallen asleep on his bunk on the north end of the kitchen.

"I'd sure like to get you a Christmas present, Barbara," he said huskily. "But you can see the state of our finances. Or lack of them."

Barbara moistened her dry lips. "It's certainly a far cry from the Christmas balls and parties on the plantation a few years back! But—" she flung out her hands. "Charlie, we love each other, and I guess that's what really matters. Sure, I could do with so many things, but I . . . I'll survive." Her voice faltered a little. "If it weren't so terribly lonely."

"I wish we could do something for Willie," Charlie said with a solemn nod. "He . . . my brother has lost so much! I didn't do him, or you either, a favor by dragging you both out here to the wild, wild West."

Instantly, Barbara pushed away her selfish thoughts. "You did what you felt was best, Charlie. Although I can't say I agree with you, this was best."

"Yes, but I wanted *space*. Now that I have plenty of it, I'm not so sure it's what I'm really after.

Barbara got up and placed her arms around his sagging shoulders. "What is it you want, Charlie?" Her voice was low.

He covered her small white hand with his broad palm. "I want a place where I can raise cattle, lots of them. Is that so wrong?"

She nuzzled her cheek against his dark curls. "I . . . don't think so. But what's the real problem?"

"Barbara," Charlie sighed. "I'm beginning to wonder if this is the best place for a ranch. It's as you said, so blasted lonely, for you and Willie. He needs boys his own age as he grows up, and you need women you can neighbor with. I can't even afford to give you a decent Christmas."

Tears lurked in Barbara's lustrous blue eyes. She saw the

hunger in his face and sensed his feeling of inadequacy to provide for them, and she choked back a sob. He was right. It *was* infernally lonely. If it weren't so far and the winters unpredictable, they might have gone to Marion Centre for a few days.

In the cold brittle days that followed, Barbara wracked her brain to think of something to give Willie for Christmas. *I can't even knit a cap or a pair of mittens*, she chided herself. She felt like a dud. *Why didn't I learn anything?*

The long winter days dragged by as the bitter winds blasted over the plains. Now and then a letter came from Marion Centre. Barbara almost ate up the news. Bitsy wrote that Mindy Harris' Lucy was getting married.

"We were around all the time when her fella courted her. Never said one word to her. He must've talked to her in Injun language! Must've hobnobbed with Silas Locklin!" Barbara's heart lifted as she chuckled out loud at Bitsy's typical humor.

A few days before Christmas, Barbara laid her school book on the table and peered out of the east window, for she'd heard the snorting of horses in the yard. Was it another mover wagon? So few had come through lately. Sometimes she wondered what had happened to the Harnishes. They had disappeared as though swallowed up in some obscure distance.

Charlie had lugged in a basketful of buffalo chips for the stove and sat down at the table to help Willie improve his penmanship.

At the stomping by the door, Henry Probst, his face like a frosty red apple under his fur cap, came in. He drew off his gloves and reached into his big pockets.

"I come vit' mail from Fort Larned. The stage left it there." He tossed several letters on the table.

Barbara pounced upon the first envelope eagerly. "It's from Callie and Lucas!" she cried, tearing it open. She smoothed out the crumpled pages and read aloud:

"We got to Lamar safe and sound, but none too soon. It's a good thing Lucas was here to deliver our big bouncin' boy. We're calling him Jason for his grandpa. Everything's fine, and Lucas has work with a blacksmith. We found a small house. It's crowded but we manage. The children are in school and I'm boardin' the schoolmaster. It brings in extra money. Lucas is so good to take all of us in but I know he worries about money. It don't look like we'll get to the mines for awhile. The least I can do is to cook extra for the teacher. It helps a little. Thanks *so much* for suggesting Lucas and I get married. It works out real good."

Barbara paused and sighed dreamily. "I'm glad we could help them when we did," she said, her voice husky.

Charlie laughed. "Well, actually we have Mame to thank for the suggestion!"

"Yah, Mame, she is a goot woman. She always says prayer for me to God." He scowled then went on. "She says you must come over on Christmas. We spend the day togedder, yah?" he added.

"Tell her we'll be delighted to come," Charlie said before Barbara could open her mouth. "I'll see if I can catch another bird or two to bring along."

"Goot. We look for you on Christmas," Henry said as he moved to the door.

After he left, Barbara turned to Charlie and frowned. "I'm not so sure going to the Probsts is such a good idea."

"Why not, Barbara?"

"Well, you know how nosey she is. She has to know everything! Besides, she simply takes over and she never asks how I feel about anything!"

"I thought you said you were lonely, Barbara. To spend a day chatting with another woman—"

"*She* does the talking, Charlie!" Barbara flared. "All I do is nod my head meekly . . . Oh, Charlie, must we go?"

Willie threw down his books. "It'll be good to get away from these confounded fractions for a change! At least we'll have Christmas away from this lonely soddy."

Barbara caught the wistful tone of his voice. *I never dreamed he felt so cooped up*, she thought. Well, spending a day with the obstreperous Mame wouldn't be easy, but she would do it for Willie and Charlie.

"I . . . I guess I can tolerate her for one day. Now I must bake gingerbread. That'll be your Christmas present, Willie. Shall I make some gingerbread men?"

"Not on your life!" Willie snorted. "Just a big flat cake. We'll take it along to Henry and Mame. I'd like to share somethin' with them. They've been mighty good to us."

"And I'd better bundle up and look for another bird," Charlie said, reaching for his heavy coat as he picked up his rifle from behind the door.

Barbara busied herself whipping up eggs with molasses for gingerbread, remembering past Christmases. Maybe if she imagined herself watching Mammy Crissy at the plantation twining festoons of red ribbons around the banisters of the winding stairway, and the gifts piled under the popcorn-entwined evergreen, she'd forget about the bleakness of the plains. Then she jerked with a start. It was gone. The big, beautiful plantation house had burned to the ground before she left Atlanta.

She shook her head violently, and brushed a tear from her eye, leaving a smudge of flour on her cheek. *I've got to go on*, she told herself grimly. *Christmas on the prairies is different. We escaped from the fire . . . and I ought to remember the way Uncle Daniel and Aunt Prudy celebrated Christmas in simplicity. And I must remember the real reason for celebrating Christmas. If Jesus hadn't been born in a lonely soddy* . . . she caught herself . . . *in a lowly stable. Oh, Lord, why am I so full of fears?*

Charlie came in with a pair of grouse which he had shot, bearing one triumphantly in each hand.

"Look! I got two birds. Can you fix them with sage stuffing?"

Sage stuffing? That was something Aggie hadn't taught her. She'd fix some cornbread dressing and toss in a bit of sage. Maybe that would do it.

Christmas morning dawned clear and brittle. The windows of the tiny bedroom were opaque from a glaze of ice. Barbara dressed hurriedly and busied herself in the kitchen. Several hours later, she eyed the two grouse with satisfaction in the enameled cooking pot. They'd turned out golden brown, with lots of thick juice to baste the crisp skin. All she needed was to pop them into Mame's oven to warm them up for dinner.

When Willie came in from the barn he grinned shyly. Drawing a tattered package from his jacket pocket, he handed it to Barbara.

"Merry Christmas, Barbara. It ain't much but . . . I had to give you somethin' . . . to my best sister and favorite teacher!"

She took the pathetically wrapped little box from his hand and opened the newspaper wrap. A doohickey of some sort made of owl feathers startled her and her eyes widened. She had no idea what it was supposed to be.

"Th . . . thanks, Willie. But . . . what is it?"

He chuckled. "I guess it's a bit hard to figger out, ain't it? Well it's meant to be a pincushion for when you patch our clothes. I'm not sure why I added the feathers, except they was so purty."

"Oh," Barbara choked back tears of gratefulness. "Why, Willie, it's . . . it's very nice. I'll always treasure it. But all I have for you is the gingerbread."

"And that's about my most special food, anyhow. How'd you guess?"

Willie was being kind and tactful and she knew it. She gave him a warm hug. "I'm so glad you like it. I tried to make it as I saw Aggie do, with flour and buttermilk and a bit of salt, ginger and molasses." It *had* turned out quite well. Maybe Mame wouldn't find fault with it and the grouse this time. Perhaps she would say something nice about Barbara's cooking for a change.

Just then Charlie stomped into the kitchen with a blast of cold air. "What? You people aren't ready? The team's rarin' to go."

Barbara hurried into the bedroom and pulled on her shabby green bombazine and brushed her blowsy hair, the brown ringlets escaping from above her ears. Her clothes were worn almost to rags from constant scrubbings, but she'd tried to save the dress she'd worn at their wedding for "best." She rummaged through the little jewelry box and found a pair of her mother's gold earrings and an amber brooch. *Why am I dressing up for Mame Probst?* she thought. It was Christmas Day. Besides, she was doing it as much for Charlie and Willie. It was an excuse to feel "merry," she reminded herself.

Bundling into her old brown coat, she tied the red wool scarf over her head.

"Let's go!" she cried gaily. *I'll enjoy myself if it kills me,* she decided.

The ride to the Probst dugout was short. Icy fingers of wind blew from the north and touched Barbara's nose playfully. As the team pulled up before the dugout, tantalizing aromas from Mame's kitchen rushed out to meet them. Charlie carried the pot with the two grouse and Willie proudly held his gingerbread high as Mame opened the door. When they stepped inside, the shoulder of venison Mame lifted from the oven dwarfed Barbara's grouse in both size and delicacy. So much for trying to keep up with Mame Probst.

Mame bounced toward Barbara and gave her a warm hug. "It's nice you come out," she chattered, turning back to the stove. "Weather's gonna turn nasty after the first. It always does. Good thing you come today. Nothin' like celebratin' Christmas together. That's what neighbors is for, ain't it?"

"As long as we remember we're celebrating Christ's birth," Barbara said.

"I've been singing 'Glory to God in the Highest' all morning. It's such a special day, havin' friends like you!"

Barbara pressed her lips together. *All right, I might as well agree.*

Mame scooped a kettle full of steamed dried corn, swimming with fresh butter and clotted cream into a blue side dish. Then she heaped a bowl high with mashed potatoes. Dots of butter ran in puddles in the generous depression. To Barbara the meal was a feast, and she knew Charlie and Willie enjoyed it, too. *I'll never match her food*, she decided.

The table, crowded into the middle of the room between the bed and kitchen shelves, was set with a mixture of cracked crockery and Staffordshire china. The tablecloth was fresh and clean and ironed to neatly creased perfection. Obviously Mame took her invitation for company seriously.

After Henry's brief table prayer of "God bless this food to Thy glory and Christmas. Amen," the small company began their holiday meal. It had been so long since they'd eaten heartily.

"Barb'ra, how'd you manage to cook them birds 'thout the gravy simmerin' out? I noticed all you had was the big enamel kettle. That burns stuff real fast, don't it?"

Not if you watch it, Barbara thought, biting her lips. Obviously Mame didn't expect much from her.

"I . . . I just watched it," she said defensively.

"Well, you don't have much to do, I can see. Now, if you had one of them iron pots, you wouldn't have to watch your vittles every second. And they'd turn out good."

Barbara was about to respond with a biting retort when she noticed something dangling from the dugout ceiling above the table. It looked like a gray-flecked rope. Then she saw it wiggle.

"Snake!" she choked out.

Mame jumped up, grabbed the intruder, waddled to the door and flung it outside. "Happens all the time. Come down from the ceiling. Them snakes like it where it's warm, you know."

"But . . . snakes in the dugout?" Barbara was aghast with fear and disgust.

"I recall as how my Aunt Tessie told when they moved to their dugout in Ioway, she said before she put the young'uns to bed durin' the hot summer, she took the beddin' outdoors every evenin' and shook out the snakes. She did it so often, she said that them snakes was friendly. They slithered away, only to come back through the roof again the next day."

Barbara closed her mouth. It was unbelievable. But then, everything about that woman defied belief.

After Willie proudly served his gingerbread, which Mame nibbled rather gingerly without comment, the woman scraped her chair and grunted to her feet. She nodded mysteriously to Henry, who went outdoors.

She turned her bulky figure and beckoned to Willie. "Seein' as you're kinda lonesome out here on the plains, boy, Henry and me, we decided to give you a present. Hope you like it. You comin', Henry?" she hollered.

Henry came back into the dugout carrying a small wiggly brown pup in his arms.

"You vant this little puppy? Our Rover, she had two babies. We can't keep both. Mame said we give this one to Villie here."

Willie's eyes grew wide and he gawked, speechless. Suddenly he squealed with laughter as he scrambled from the table and rushed for the little ball of fur. The joy that shone in his face was incredible. Barbara knew it was a gift no one could have topped.

Nuzzling the warm, brown head against his cheek, Willie crooned over and over: "Mogie . . . Mogie . . . Mogie. . . "

On the way home later, with Willie cuddling his pup in his arms in the straw behind them, Charlie turned to Barbara.

"I'm sorry you didn't have a good time—especially when that snake sort of spoiled things. But I thought you needed to get away from our cabin. I really meant well, my darling."

She drew a long, cold breath. "I don't know what's worse— the loneliness, or the unpalatable Mame! But after her gift to Willie, I can almost forgive her for the snake and for the tart remarks about not cooking my food in an iron pot! I'll never match her cooking. At least Aggie was nice about my mishaps."

Charlie threw back his head and laughed. "That's my Barbara. I knew you'd come around sooner or later."

I'm not so sure I've "come around" as Charlie says, she thought. But the day had been something to think about. She wondered if the wise men's gifts to the Christmas child had been received with any more joy than Willie's gift of the wiggly brown puppy!

CHAPTER 10

*T*he year of 1866 stomped in with Mame's predictions of a winter storm. All afternoon it had grown dark with too-early blackness. Low scudding clouds now rolled over the plains, boiling and hissing like a belligerent giant with huge, inflated cheeks and pursed, angry lips that snarled with rage. Sleet flung icy crystals against the tiny windows.

As Charlie stomped in from the barns, a blinding blast of snow-filled wind blew through the open door and hurled the icy crystals like blowing sand across the floor. Barbara cowered by the topsy stove, trying to soak up the bursts of warmth that snorted from the grate.

"Sure's a bad one," Charlie muttered, slapping his hands together. "I guess winter's arrived with a vengeance."

Barbara shivered in the shabby brown jacket she'd pulled over her faded pink gingham. "Will it storm like this all day?" she asked. "It's almost too cold for Willie's schooling."

"These storms can leave as suddenly as they blow in. Again, they can last for days. Remember last year at Marion Centre? We shoveled snow for weeks."

She scowled, remembering the constant clink of shovels and stomp of snow-crusted boots as the men struggled to clear paths to the barns to look after the stock. She had survived the winter and she would now, she supposed. But sometimes she wondered if she'd ever be warm again.

She kept a pot of beef soup simmering on the stove, the heady aroma drifting through the soddy. Its soothing bubble seemed to take the edge from the ice-tipped blizzard that raged outdoors.

"Well, at least the Injuns won't do any rampagin' in this weather," Willie chortled, curled up on his bunk with Mogie. The boy and the dog were never apart. Whenever Willie reluctantly tackled his schoolwork, the little brown pup always lay sprawled at his feet. Barbara smiled at the pair. Willie seemed totally content with his Christmas gift from Mame and Henry.

"What makes you mention Indians, Willie?" she asked idly.

"Oh, Henry claims he seen a few bucks on an antelope hunt last week," Willie's voice was nonchalant, and Barbara's shivers weren't entirely from the cold. She was never quite comfortable with Indians in the area. Of course, they were much more active along the Smoky Hill.

Fuel was growing scarce. With the snow covering the prairies, Charlie had been unable to find as many buffalo chips as before. The bitter cold weather seemed to defy the topsy's struggle to keep the cabin warm. With little wood on the treeless plains, there was a constant battle for survival to appease the little stove's giant appetite.

The storm finally broke and the prairie lay still and white as a dead man in his shroud.

Willie often read his lessons aloud, more for Mogie's benefit than for Barbara's, she suspected. But she was satisfied that his reading skills had improved. Somewhere among the books he'd dug out of the trunk was a copy of Whittier's *Snowbound*. The story itself provoked icy fingers down Barbara's back.

She washed a few shirts and dresses and hung them up to dry on a rope Charlie had stretched across the kitchen, and the house grew steamy and beaded the windows with sweat. In the simple household tasks of cooking, mending and teaching, she resigned herself to stay indoors huddling near the warmth of the stove.

One evening when Charlie came in from the barns, he tossed his jacket into a corner and went into a fit of coughing.

"Lucky . . . the war's over," he sputtered after another spasm of wheezing. "If the . . . soldiers . . . had to hole up . . . in their winter quarters . . . this kind of weather."

"Charlie, what's wrong? Are you sick?" Barbara cried, alarmed at the sudden onslaught of coughing. He'd been out for days tramping through deep snows in the biting cold with boots that had grown thin where the leather had almost worn through. That Charlie, always strong and stalwart, was now keeling under to the wintry blasts, seemed so inconceivable. She had felt he would endure forever.

As he sagged into a chair, Barbara noticed how pale his usually tanned face had become.

"I . . . I guess I caught . . . a bit of cold," he sputtered. "This weather's not tolerable . . . for bucking snowdrifts."

Barbara was at his side instantly. Placing her arms around him, she drew his head against her shoulders. She glanced anxiously at Willie. He must have read the deep concern in her eyes, for he jumped up quickly and laid Mogie on his bunk.

"I'll fix up your bed nice and warm with hot bricks, Charlie," he said, hurrying about the room, "while Barbara stirs up somethin' for you to drink. Then you go to bed."

"But the fuel . . . the animals," Charlie burst into another fit of coughing.

"Don't worry. I'll take over until you feel better."

While Barbara fixed some hot milk laced generously with honey, Willie heated bricks and carried them to the bedroom. Then he gently unlaced Charlie's boots and pulled them off.

When he had gulped down the hot milk, Willie and Barbara led him into the bedroom and helped him to bed.

She covered him up, after carefully arranging the hot bricks as comfortably near his feet as she could. Then she leaned over and kissed him.

"Now take a good long nap, Charlie. After you wake up you'll feel better. Mammy Crissy always insisted one could 'sleep off' a bad cold."

She motioned to Willie and they left the bedroom. The kitchen had grown cold as the embers in the topsy stove had died down. She carefully threw in more chips. Then she sank into the one good chair at the table and laid her head on her arms.

"Oh, Willie," she whispered, "I'm afraid Charlie's awfully sick. What can we do?"

"Do you remember what Aunt Prudy did when Rosie and John's little Sammy had the lung fever?"

"Lung fever?" Barbara echoed. She jerked up her head. Had Charlie's cold already turned into the dreaded pneumonia?

"She . . . she cut onions into thin slices and sprinkled sugar between each layer and let it stand for an hour, although I knew she also made a poultice of the onions. I believe she baked them but I don't remember quite how she did it. I guess I didn't learn *anything*!"

"Do we have any more onions in the cellar?"

She shook her head. "I used up the last we had for the dressing we fixed for the grouse. Oh, Willie, why didn't I save some?"

Willie stood before her, his hands behind his back. "Well, keep Charlie good and warm. Maybe by mornin' his fever will break and he'll be fine. Why don't you go to bed? I'll stay up and tend to the fire awhile.

Wearily Barbara made her way to the tiny bedroom, took off her faded gingham and slipped into the flannel nightgown. Before she crawled into bed with Charlie, she knelt down.

"Oh, Lord," she cried softly, "You know what a fix we're in, and so far from any help, and Charlie so sick. If only Grandma Griffith was here. Please, please dear Lord, send us the help we need. We've trusted You all these months and You've never let us down. We ask again for Your help."

What more can I do but commit my gravely ill husband into the Lord's keeping?

If "sleeping off the fever" had worked in the South, it wasn't happening on the Kansas plains in the dead of winter. Charlie tossed and turned, moaning and coughing until Barbara despaired of being able to bring relief. Touching Charlie's forehead with her hand, she knew he was burning with fever. There was no doubt. Charlie had the dreaded lung fever that took its toll of babies and grownups every winter on the prairies. She knew lung fever got into the chest and burned until one could no longer breathe.

When morning broke at last, Barbara dressed hurriedly and went to the kitchen. Willie was already up, stoking the fire and bundling himself into Charlie's warm coat.

"Wind's died down. I'll go out and look after the chores, and bring in more chips. Hope our little pile will last for awhile."

Barbara nodded mutely. He would have to take care of Charlie's work while she nursed her husband.

A sudden idea hit her. "After you've chored, Willie, why not ride to Fort Larned and see if the company doctor could come out? Maybe he can do something with his supply of medicines."

"I'll hurry with the milkin', Barbara, so's I can get away sooner. You just look after my brother and don't worry. The Lord'll take care of us." With the slam of the kitchen door he was gone.

Barbara rushed into the bedroom and checked on Charlie. His face was flushed and covered with sweat. Dear God, what can I do? I've never been so frightened in my life! He looked so pale and drawn and there was no flicker of recognition in his summer-blue eyes.

"My dear, wonderful Charlie," she whispered. "Please, please don't leave us! Please get better. We need you!"

Amid praying and chafing his hands between her own, Barbara tried to rouse him, but there was no response.

The minute she heard Willie slam the kitchen door she flew to meet him.

"Willie, Willie," she cried, "Charlie, he doesn't say anything. He . . . he's very sick. Please . . . please ride as fast as you can to the fort. I'll take care of everything here!"

He warmed his hands, gulped down a glass of warm milk, and grabbed a crust of bread.

"Take good care, Barbara. I'll be back soon as I can. Keep the topsy hot and heat them bricks. And," he fumbled in his pocket, "here's a bottle of whiskey I found in the shed. Charlie told me once it was good for a cold. Stir in some honey and make him swaller it. I'm off now." With a hug for Mogie, he hurried out of the house. Mogie followed him to the door with a whimper.

She watched Willie ride away on Duke, plunging through the crusted drifts to the small rail gate. Far up the snow-packed road he galloped, his arms high so that the gray shawl she'd insisted he take, formed wings. Through her tears she thought he looked like a big gray moth flying into the cold winter sky.

She patted Mogie's head. He had stopped whimpering. "I've got to help Charlie," she said to the pup who wagged his stubby tail.

Gingerly she picked up the bottle of whiskey, poured a cup half full and stirred in a generous dose of honey. Then she carried it to the bedroom.

Charlie had flung off the covers and his glazed eyes seemed faintly lucid. She knelt down and held the cup to his lips.

"Please, Charlie," she said softly. "Please drink this. Maybe it will help. I . . . used some of the whiskey you'd saved for colds. Willie's gone for the doctor."

Charlie choked on the whiskey and flung the cup away from himself until it shattered onto the floor. "Bar . . ." his voice was slurred. "So hot in here . . ."

Dear God, what do I do now? she thought wildly. Remembering the time she had nursed Willie when he had burned with a fever of diphtheria, she recalled having tried to keep his forehead cool with towels dipped in cold water.

Hurrying back to the kitchen, she grabbed a pail, stepped outside and clawed several handfuls of snow from the stone slab by the door. As she poured water on the snow, it grew sharp and cold. She dipped a towel into it, wrung it out and placed it on Charlie's forehead.

"Oh, Charlie, maybe this will help," she muttered. He had

grown unconscious again and she hurried back to make another cold compress. She continued to nurse him by trying to cool his feverish brow and shoulders in a continual cycle of gathering snow, wringing towels and changing compresses.

Glancing at the clock, she noticed Willie had been gone for hours. If only the doctor would hurry.

Fear washed over her in great waves. She couldn't face life without Charlie. *And to think I hated him once,* she grimaced. She knelt down and prayed again. From somewhere a verse in Isaiah came to her: *"Thou wilt keep him in perfect peace whose mind is stayed on thee: because he trusteth in thee . . ."*

"Oh, Lord, maybe I've not trusted enough. Please forgive me! I just can't . . . think."

Charlie began to cough again. Barbara bent over him and stroked his forehead. It was so hot. *Dear God, when will the fever break?*

Just then she thought she heard the thunder of horses' hooves. Willie and the doctor! She jumped up, rushed to the kitchen and flung open the door. Willie was alone.

Through frozen lips he whispered, "Doctor . . . couldn't come. Out on another call. But I stopped at Henry and Mame's. She'll be here . . . directly."

"Mame Probst?" Barbara gasped. She couldn't stand that woman. *What was the matter with Willie?* A spurt of anger stirred as a sense of hopelessness swept over her. *What could big, blurry Mame Probst do that she hadn't already done?*

CHAPTER 11

*W*ith a sigh Barbara calmed. Hadn't she prayed for help? Had God sent this obstreperous woman who took over and pushed herself into the way where she wasn't wanted?

Before Willie had warmed up in front of the topsy stove and cuddled Mogie for a few minutes, Mame clattered up on her old mule, swaddled in layers of coats and scarves. As she pattered into the kitchen, she slammed a covered basket on the table.

"Here, I've everthin' we need to fight the battle." She began to pull out one thing after another. "Onions for poultice. Mustard for plaster. Goose grease. Dried dandelion leaves and some curly dock and wild mustard for tonics. And cambric for tea. Now let's get to work." Before she had finished speaking she was peeling away the layers of scarves and coats until she stood stout as a barrel in the middle of the kitchen in her dark blue percale. In a moment she had tied a huge gray apron around her ample waist. Barbara noticed the determined gleam in the faded gray eyes, and somehow a faint breath of hope stirred in her bosom.

"You keep the stove red and hot water goin'," Mame ordered Barbara, who could only stand by silently and blink. "Boy," she called to Willie, "you help me slice this pan full of onions to bake for a poultice. If that don't help, we'll fix a mustard

79

plaster. Now, let's get movin'."

The kitchen grew redolent with the strong scent of onions as Mame cut and chopped. After she shoved the pan full of onions into the oven, she turned to Barbara.

"Here. Take this warm goose grease and rub it on Charlie's chest. Now rub it *hard* so it will warm clean through to his lungs. As soon's the onions is baked, I'll bring in the poultice."

Like a wooden doll, Barbara picked up the pan of goose grease Mame had warmed on the back of the stove and went into the bedroom. Too frightened to think clearly, she knelt down and pulled away Charlie's blankets. He coughed a few times and tried to push her away.

"Charlie, I want to help you!" she pleaded, tears cutting shiny paths down her cheeks. "Please lie still!"

His unbleached night shirt was soaked with sweat as she opened the buttons. Tossing and turning, he thrashed around wildly whenever she tried to rub his chest.

"Charlie, please!" she cried. Her rising voice must have reached Mame in the kitchen who lumbered into the bedroom and pushed her aside without a word. Her strong, capable fingers held Charlie's arms tightly as she spoke gruffly.

"Now, listen, Mister Warren. If you had half the sense you was born with, you'd lay back and let us help you. How'd you 'spect your wife and brother to live here alone if you don't let us fix you up? Now, do I have to cuff you, or do you let us help?"

As though Charlie was aware of gruff commands, his flagging arms grew still.

His face looked so haggard, so sallow that fear clutched Barbara's heart again. *Was he . . . was he still alive?*

"You keep massagin', Honey. Them onions should be bout ready now," Mame ordered curtly, and swept from the room.

Tears spilling down her cheeks, Barbara rubbed his throat, and his chest that now rattled with phlegm, praying silently as she worked. At times his breath came so fast and hoarse that it sounded like a whistle made from the willows that fringed the Cottonwood River near Marion Centre.

Her long brown hair had loosed from its pins and sagged down her back. She bunched it up hastily and stuck the pins back into a slouchy bun.

Mame marched into the bedroom carrying a pan of the onion poultice. With rough, red fingers, she adjusted the bag of onions on Charlie's chest. He had grown very quiet, and Barbara looked at Mame anxiously.

"He's in a coma now," the woman said brusquely. "Let's leave him rest while the onion poultice does its work. C'mon." She grabbed Barbara's arm and literally dragged her into the kitchen.

Willie stood at the east window, looking through the ice-scraped pane, Mogie in his arms. He didn't seem aware that they had come into the kitchen.

"The boy's plum tuckered out from the long ride to the fort," Mame mumbled in a low voice. "Willie, git away from that winder and crawl under your covers. You git some rest afore it's time to chore."

Willie meekly followed Mame's orders. Obviously Mame expected to be obeyed. But then, she expected everyone to do as she commanded. That was what had irked Barbara about her from the beginning. Instead of being firm and gentle as Aunt Prudy had been, this woman had the knack of taking over and bossing. She never seemed to have a good word for anyone. *She's gritty as sandpaper,* Barbara told herself.

Yet Barbara had to admit to herself, underneath all that bluster and guff, Mame Probst had a heart. *I've just been too blind to see it,* she chided herself.

Somehow she allowed Mame to push her into a kitchen chair. From somewhere in the mysterious innards of the basket, Mame pulled out a dried apple pie.

"Here, let me cut you a piece. I bet you ain't had a bit to eat all day, have you?" Placing a slice of pie onto a saucer, she shoved it toward Barbara.

"No, no," Barbara shook her head. "I . . . I can't eat. As long as Charlie's so sick—"

"Hesh up now. Mame's here and Charlie needs a strong

woman, not a sniveling little wench. I made some coffee, too. It's settin' on the back of the stove. Just you set back and relax with this bit of lunch while I go back into the bedroom." With that she bounced away like an oversized rubber ball.

Barbara stirred her coffee idly and nibbled at the pie. It was every bit as good as Aggie's, she had to admit, and there was much about Mame that was good.

Lord, she prayed silently, *Forgive me for being so loathe to see her huge, gentle heart. I've been so selfish—*

"He's holdin' his own, Barb'ra," Mame was at her elbow. "Maybe we'll win the fight with the good Lord's help."

"Then you believe God will hear our prayers? I've prayed and prayed—"

"Of course He hears us, child. He ain't deaf! That's not sayin' He's gonna always give us what we ask for."

"But I don't know what I'd do without Charlie! He's so wonderful—"

"The good Lord knows exactly what you need, child. Just leave it to Him. Ain't He our lovin' Savior?"

"Then you believe He died for our sins, Mame?" Barbara prodded. "I wasn't sure if you were a believer."

"He saved me a long time ago when I was a child and called upon His name," the blurry woman said, taking another pan full of onions from the oven. "But now, take Henry. Well, he was raised in a real strict home in Germany with his own religion. He's so stubborn, can't see that it took Jesus Christ to die for our sins to redeem us. He pertends to believe but I 'spect he does it to please me. But grace is the only way we can get to heaven, you know."

Barbara nodded. So many settlers seemed religious, but Barbara suspected some used religion as a crutch because of their fear of the unknown. She hadn't known of the crusty woman's faith. Yet it warmed her heart to know that in spite of her gruff exterior, Mame loved the Lord.

"Well, we'll have to keep showing Henry that God loves him," Barbara ventured. "It took me a long time to see that. It wasn't until Matthew died . . . Matthew was my fiance who was killed in battle . . . and then God took Rosie and John's little Sammie. Yet Uncle Daniel's family's faith was never shaken, in spite of all the things that happened to them."

"You was lucky you had such good folks. My Henry's awful stubborn, though he's a good man."

Mame motioned to Barbara and together they went to the bedroom. Charlie seemed asleep, but Mame was cautious.

"He ain't turned the corner yet. Help me put this poultice on. In another hour or so we'll see."

When they returned to the kitchen, Willie was bundling into his coat. He picked up the milk pails and headed for the door. Then he turned.

"I just noticed the icicles are drippin' from the roof," he said "Maybe it's warmin' a little."

If the cold let up and the snow melted, everything would be easier to manage. An hour later Charlie still lay white and feverish. Mame shook her head slightly.

"He ain't comin' out of his newmony like he should. We'll try the mustard plaster. You got hog lard? And red flannel?"

"The lard is in that tin on the shelf," Barbara said, her heart leaping with fear at Mame's grim words. "As for red flannel—"

"Never mind." Mame spun around and Barbara heard a ripping sound. When the woman turned back, she had a generous piece of red flannel petticoat in her hands. Tears stung Barbara's eyes. *Was there no end to Mame's brusque goodness? I'd better learn something this time,* she decided.

"Mame, how do you make a mustard plaster?" she asked helplessly. *I must sound awfully stupid,* she thought.

Mame was already at the table. "Take two tablespoons of hog lard, a spoonful of ground mustard, and mix it good. Smooth it on red wood flannel and lay it on the chest. It's awful strong. But it's real easy. Here. Why don't you lay it on Charlie now and see if that'll do the trick? But take off the poultice first."

On legs that shook, Barbara carried the plaster into the bedroom and gently removed the baked onion poultice.

"Dear Lord," she whispered, "Let the mustard plaster help!"

Charlie lay with his eyes closed, but the wheezing in his

chest had stopped. She placed the mustard plaster on the thin chest and leaned over to kiss him. He looked so pitiful and dear. How could she give him up? What had Mame said? That God didn't always give us what we asked for? With a lump in her throat, she prayed "Lord, whatever's best, please let me accept it." She choked out the words in a voice thick with tears.

As night came on, Mame was still there, her plump figure bouncing around in the kitchen. Barbara was silent now. She had told the Lord what she really didn't believe, but to do what was best. She couldn't bear to tell Willie who had stumbled into bed as soon as he'd wolfed down a heaping bowl of Mame's rabbit stew. He'd been very quiet. Barbara knew he hurt so deeply.

Mame seated herself beside Charlie's bed, and Barbara stood at the foot end. Outside she could hear the drip-drip of water from the eaves and knew the cold wind had died and the ice was melting. The candle guttered on the apple crate stand beside the bed in the sudden gust of wind through the panes.

As the night dragged on without a sound from the bed, Barbara threw herself on her knees beside Charlie and clasped one of his hot hands in hers. She felt utterly numb and broken.

She must have fallen asleep on her knees, when suddenly she felt someone shaking her shoulders.

"Barb'ra Honey. I think you better wake up."

Opening her eyes wide, she stared at Charlie's face in the feeble light of the candle and blinked.

His eyes were wide open, and a faint grin touched his sallow cheeks. Then she knew he'd "turned the corner," as Mame would say. She threw her arms around him and hugged him tightly.

"Oh, Charlie, Charlie, you're going to be all right, aren't you?" she cried.

"Couldn't leave . . . you alone quite yet, could I?" he said in a ragged voice. "I . . . love you . . . too much, darling. You know that!"

She began to cry with great heaving sobs of joy and relief.

The tears were dripping over the covers. She noticed Mame had left the bedroom. With a quick nod toward Charlie, Barbara got up and hurried to the kitchen.

Dawn was breaking in the east, and its feeble rays stole soft and pink over the horizon as icicles dripped noisily from the roof. Mame was quietly packing up her gear into the basket.

"Oh, Mame," Barbara cried. "Must you go? It's so early."

"You don't need me anymore, Honey. It's time I got back to Henry. Willie's already saddlin' my mule."

"I'll always need you, Mame. More than I ever dreamed . . . I . . . I—"

"That's what neighbors is for. Don't you know that by now?" The woman had bundled herself in her layers of coats, then paused with a jar in her hand.

"This is cambric tea. See that Charlie gets lots of it." Without another word she padded out the kitchen door. Barbara realized suddenly how much she'd counted on Mame's comforting presence.

For a moment her heart pounded with gratefulness. She knew without a doubt that it was Mame Probst's faithful nursing that had saved Charlie's life. More than that, she remembered her prayer, *Do what's best, Lord.* With a surge of joy, she knew God had used Mame to do the job.

CHAPTER 12

March came in like neither a lion nor a lamb; but rather like an ox—stolid and plodding. The winds no longer gusted across the bare plains in cold fury. The snows had finally melted in the warm spring winds and trickled away to soak the brown grasses. Wild geese honking on the banks of Turkey Creek were the first harbingers of warmer weather. Spring was on the horizon.

Charlie's convalescence had been long and tedious, and for the first time in weeks he had gone outdoors to check the animals. Willie had fed the stock and searched for chips to feed the ever-hungry stove. Henry Probst had stopped by faithfully. He had shown Willie some dried saplings along the creek for fuel.

Barbara rummaged through Aunt Prudy's boxes of garden seeds and read each little packet with interest. Her aunt had scribbled quaint little notes on each tiny sack: GR. BEENS—plant mid April; PEES—earlyer the better; TOMATOS—when forst is pasted.

Dear Aunt Prudy! She'd wanted to be sure the seeds were planted at the proper time. Willie insisted potatoes must be planted on St. Patrick's Day, even if it snows.

The rose bush cutting had taken root and a few green shoots covered the prickly spines. The prospect of garden fresh food on the table made Barbara's mouth water. She'd cried when Mame Probst had brought over her first gathering of wild greens.

"Cook 'em with chunk of salt pork, Honey. They's lots of good eatin' in a mess . . . 'specially if cooked in an iron pot."

Mame knew full well that Barbara had only gray enameled cookware, but with her usual lack of tact she jabbed her with the reminder. It was Mame's way, Barbara reminded herself tartly.

As Charlie planted corn and oats, Willie dug up the garden spot just west of the cabin. Then he raked it smooth and helped Barbara tamp in the seeds as per Aunt Prudy's cryptic notes. He chuckled over the "forst is pasted," which they translated as "frost is past."

The spring rains had been gentle, and soon the flat, tawny acres were checkered with squares of green. Before long, tiny garden vegetables shot up in the little plot of ground.

Charlie came in one evening with a more-than-usual bounce in his step. "The Parkers have moved into a soddy just down the Trail," he announced after Barbara's quick kiss. "There are three children and another on the way. The woman looks plenty tired out. I told them we'd have a get-together some Sunday afternoon, maybe even start a church service sometimes, if the Reverend Sternberg comes this way from Ellsworth."

"Do you still have that ol' accordion?" Willie asked. "You used to play it when we lived in Illinois."

"Well, I think it's stashed somewhere in the shed. Prob'ly covered with dust. I packed it in a sack of oats, I remember."

"Charlie!" Barbara cried. "I didn't know you played one of those squeeze boxes!"

He threw back his head and laughed, "If you call my wrenching out those agonizing chords, playing!"

"Oh, it ain't that bad," Willie put in. "Well, with the Evans family movin' up by the river and the Parkers—we'll soon have a settlement here."

Barbara pressed her lips together. Real "settlements"

weren't scattered far out like the soddies here on the plains. Yet this could be the beginning of her war against loneliness. God knew she needed it.

"Let's plan a get-together next Sunday afternoon." Charlie suggested. "What do you say darling?"

"If you think the newcomers will come."

"'Course they will!" Willie burst out. "I guess the women will be tickled to death to meet ya. And Henry and Mame'll be here, you may be sure. I'll ride out Saturday afternoon and hand out the invites. Sure you don't want 'em engraved in gold?" His blue eyes twinkled.

It had been so long since Barbara had entertained guests that she immediately thought of the ever-present need of feeding them. That could pose a problem, for their supplies were running low again.

"Well, sure. I . . . what will we feed them?" she blurted finally. "We barely have enough—"

"Never mind. Everyone'll bring food. Besides, don't worry. Just gettin' together will satisfy most everyone," Charlie put in sagely.

On Saturday Barbara scrubbed floors and washed the kitchen curtains which had become dingy with the winter's soot and smoke of the stove. She sent Willie outdoors to beat the braided rugs. She aired the pillows and quilts by hanging them on the clothesline after the dust from the rugs had settled.

"Who's gonna sniff your beddin', Barbara?" he grumbled. "You expectin' President Andrew Johnson?"

"Oh, go on, Willie," she snapped. "If I'm going to entertain the entire settlement, I'd better be prepared for anyone!"

Charlie had shot and cleaned several prairie chickens and Barbara dipped them in cornmeal and fried them crisp and crusty. She picked and podded the first new peas. Then she boiled a big kettle filled with them and dabbed fresh butter on top. The long pan full of spoon bread was cooling on the table. It had taken more cornmeal than she felt she could spare, but she didn't want the newcomers to feel cheated. Now to wash her hair and iron her dress.

At two o'clock Sunday afternoon, a wagon creaked up the lane. Barbara, wearing her second best blue lawn, felt her heart hammer with anticipation. How would the women respond to her? She probably looked frowsy and countrified after the past harsh months in the West.

The Parkers were the first to arrive. Eva Mae, her cheap brown percale skirt billowing from her ballooning waistline, clambered over the wheel and trotted to the door as soon as the wagon pulled to a stop. As she jerked off her bonnet, her very young, tired face startled Barbara. The three youngsters spilled from the back of the wagon like peas from a pod.

The woman reached out her arms. "Barbara Warren, Willie never told me how purty you look! And your skin's fresh and pink as a wild rose. How do you do it in this country?"

Barbara blushed. She knew immediately that Eva Mae Parker would be her friend for life. Maybe she wasn't as frowsy as she felt.

Before they had settled down to visit, Herb and Ann Evans pulled into the yard, and Henry and Mame Probst came shortly after.

"I brought a mess of wild grape dumplin's," Mame greeted her with a warm, damp hug after she had bounced indoors carrying the inevitable iron kettle to the table. "A Kiowa Injun squaw showed me how to make it when we visited Oklahoma Territory once."

"Made of wild grapes, you say?" Plain, plump Ann Evans prodded, raising the lid for a peek. "Sure looks good. All I had on hand was a mess o' greens. We still ain't settled in."

Although the company lacked finesse and charm, Barbara found herself warming to the women more than she had thought she would.

After the visitors sat down on boxes and benches in the meager shade on the east side of the soddy, Charlie brought out his accordion.

As he coaxed wheezy chords from the dusty old instrument, he modulated into several hymns. The small congregation sang with untrained voices. Barbara saw Willie trying to stifle his laughter at Mame's shrill rendition of "Jesus Bids Us Shine" as she dragged the "Je-a-zus" from a high note down to one at the bottom of the scale.

When the group had sung all the hymns they knew, a few old ballads and folk songs followed. *It was almost like old times in Marion Centre,* Barbara thought.

She recalled the time Charlie had paired up with her at the Fourth of July picnic and they had swung around in "The Miller's Boy." She smiled, remembering in her fury she'd run away because she'd hated him then, and Vange had joshed her, saying, "Matthew had better watch out." She recalled having slapped her for that. Had God planned for her and Charlie to be married all along? How was she to know that she loved him even then? She'd almost blown her chance when Charlie and Willie were bent on heading West. And here she was—a frontier woman, perhaps not so frowsy after all, hosting a motley bunch of settlers on a Sunday afternoon on a lonely prairie.

Her thoughts had now drifted to the afternoon gathering and she pasted a smile on her face and clapped her hands as she said, "Let's all come in for a bite to eat. Mame will help me dish up."

Before long the buzz of friendly voices and clatter of flatware permeated the quiet afternoon. Rather than helping, Mame bossed the entire meal as usual. Barbara no longer minded. She'd forgiven Mame for being tactless.

After the last wagon wheel creaked away and the final goodbye echoed over the prairie, Barbara sighed. She knew they would get together again.

A week later Pete Parker rode over on his roan. "I hear Rev'rund Bowers is comin' for service. Since you have the most room, we wondered—"

"Say no more, Pete," Charlie cut in. "Of course, we'll have church here in our sodhouse." Pete smiled gratefully at Charlie's generosity.

"I guess we owe it to the Lord to provide spiritual nurture to those who hunger for it," he told Barbara later.

The days had dragged into June and summer officially arrived. Busy with the garden in the heat, Barbara cleaned and scrubbed and prepared for company again. She grew hot and sweaty long before sunset. Yet somehow she was filled with a peace she couldn't explain.

Reverend Bowers possessed a real spirit of evangelism and, as he paced back and forth in front of the topsy stove, he preached with such zeal that Mame and Henry, who were kept at home with a sick cow, claimed later they had heard him through the open windows of their dugout two miles away! The house was crowded that day, and Barbara was sure she would never forget the service. People they had never met before drove in from 15 or 20 miles away, including several soldiers from Fort Larned. She moved into the bedroom and sat on the bed.

Preacher Bowers' high-pitched voice grew shrill as he thundered, "Ye must be born again! If ye want to enter the kingdom of God, like it says in the Scriptures, you hafta confess your sins and believe Jesus died on the cross. You kin do that right now, today!"

The soddy grew suddenly very quiet as one by one, several strong-bodied, bearded men moved forward and knelt down. Prayers of repentance seemed to pierce the roof on their way to God's throne. Tears streamed down Barbara's face as she stood in the bedroom and saw God's Spirit at work in the humble little sodhouse. Charlie was right. They owed their lives to God. And to think she'd resented living in such a wild, lonely situation.

Just then she felt the floor sag. *Were the wide floorboards buckling?* Sure enough, they sagged and were threatening to give. She pushed her way unobtrusively toward Charlie who leaned in the open doorway of the cabin.

"Charlie," she whispered anxiously, "the floor's sagging. What's happening to our house?"

He gazed at her in alarm. Then without a word he tiptoed to the preacher and tapped his shoulder, interrupting the plea for sinners to come to the altar. Low murmurs drifted over

91

the little soddy at this unusual procedure.

The grizzled Reverend Bowers paused, then raised one hand to quiet the whispers.

"I better ask you all to step outside so Brother Warren can prop up the floor. It's shiftin' *way* down!" he hollered.

With a quiet shuffle, the little congregation pushed through the open doorway. Charlie and Pete Parker crawled into the small cellar and braced the floor with several stout pieces of lumber that Willie brought from behind the shed.

Half an hour later, the service resumed.

After everyone had left, Willie stood in the doorway and turned to face Charlie and Barbara who stood soberly silent after seeing off the departed guests.

"I'm not pokin' fun, mind you, but do you s'pose it was all them burdens that got dumped out here that made the floor buckle like that? And the way the preacher chased the doxology clear through the rafters! No wonder our soddy was in danger of collapsin'!"

His remarks broke their quiet composure and Barbara laughed. "If you don't sound just like Bitsy!" she chuckled.

Charlie grinned as he tweaked Barbara's nose. "Well that was a keen observation and an object lesson. Willie, you hit the ol' nail on the head."

And to Barbara, the warmth of that sunny, Sunday afternoon suddenly seemed very sacred and special.

CHAPTER 13

One hot June morning as Barbara hung out the week's wash on the rope line Charlie had stretched from the house to the barn, a blue-clad soldier clattered up the lane on his black stallion and drew to a stop beside her.

The soldier apparently came from Fort Larned. He bowed and drew off his blue cap. Barbara pushed back her damp sunbonnet and fanned her hot face as she waited for him to state his business.

"You're Miz Warren, ain't you?" he asked politely, and she nodded. He paused and fumbled in his pocket, drawing out a crumpled scrap of cloth. "Is this yours?"

As he unfolded it and held it up, she gasped. It was the cross-stitched sampler that had hung on the east wall of the soddy which had disappeared the day Liz and Clem Harnish had left. The words "God Careth For You" were smudged and dirty, but she recognized it instantly.

"Where did you find it?"

The soldier shaded his eyes against the morning sun with his cap. "We was ridin' out a ways west the other day when we came across a covered wagon. The team was gone, but inside the wagon we found the bodies of a man and woman. There was letters addressed to Clem Harnish. Most likely they froze to death last winter durin' the blizzard."

A pang shot through Barbara and she drew her breath sharply. No doubt, the Harnishes were overtaken by the storm. They'd lingered so long, not knowing where they were going.

"Where did you find the . . . sampler?" she asked again, her voice low.

"The woman was clutchin' it in her hand, like she was readin' it. It had B.T. stitched on the back and when Cap'n Frost said your name was Barb'ra, we took a chance on figurin' it maybe belonged to you. Seein' as their name was Harnish, we figured it wasn't her'n. Would you know how she got it?"

"I . . ." Barbara swallowed hard, trying to forget the painful morning when the couple had worn out their welcome. "They stopped by last fall . . . and stayed for several days. Charlie wasn't home and I thought they'd never leave. When they finally drove away, I suddenly noticed my sampler was gone. They . . . they were strange, and didn't seem to know where they were headed. I didn't know what to make of them. Willie didn't either."

"Well, they must'a been drifters. We couldn't find any sign of food in the wagon. Could'a starved to death, too. They was awfully thin."

Barbara gasped. "Then it wasn't Indians? They . . . they kept begging for something to eat. At first I was glad to have them because it was so lonely, but then they began to make me uncomfortable. I was relieved when they finally left," she said, remembering how she had connived to make the woman believe Willie had cholera. "But had I known—"

The soldier raised a hand. "These things happen, ma'am. Like I said, they was drifters, livin' off what they could snitch and beg. Lucky for you they left when they did. Well . . ." he thrust the sampler in Barbara's hands, "don't blame yourself. They might'a leeched off'a you if they hadn't left when they did, or robbed you blind." They he clucked to his horse and rode away.

Slowly Barbara turned her gaze to stare at the sampler in her hands. *I wish I didn't know the outcome of that grim story,* she thought. *But I should've told them about the Lord—and I didn't. Lord, don't let me be so insensitive again. Let my life count for you!*

When she told Charlie and Willie about it later, Willie shook his head.

"I had this weird feelin' about them right from the start. We couldn't fight their battles for them, Barbara."

"Yes, but at least I could've told them God loved them," she flared. "After the way I tried to make them leave—"

"Well, you let them know through this Bible verse on the sampler, didn't you?"

Had she? Barbara lowered her eyes. She could never be sure. If they hadn't taken the sampler, she might never had known what happened to them. Maybe that was why Charlie wanted to use their soddy as a house of worship—so others could learn of God's love.

Before the next Sunday service, Charlie made sure he had reinforced the wide board floor to hold a room full of people. At Preacher Bower's visit God had been very obviously present, and He could do it again. *If only Henry Probst had been there,* Barbara thought.

In the evening after the farm chores were done, Charlie and Willie sawed and hammered, and by morning several sturdy benches stretched across the little kitchen. Of course, they'd have to cart the table outside to make room.

As usual the little soddy was crowded Sunday afternoon with worshipers. It was a bright, clear day and Barbara noticed another new family. She learned they had come from the next county, and their name was McNeer.

When the preacher began the opening prayer, the room suddenly grew dark. Barbara, her eyes lowered, wondered if the sky had become overcast. They needed rain and perhaps it had grown cloudy. She glanced furtively to look.

To her horror, she saw Indian faces—perhaps 10 or more— peering three deep through the windows.

Oh, dear God, not Indians! She fought the rising panic in her throat. Without a word, Charlie slipped to the mantel and grabbed his gun. Her heart hammered wildly, her hands clenched in horror. Would they all be massacred before the service began? The little crowd gasped, and stirred uneasily, and Barbara saw the fright in Ann Evans' face. Henry Probst pointed to the windows, and Charlie suddenly laid down his gun and drew a deep sigh of relief.

The preacher had stopped in the middle of his prayer and looked at the leering faces in the windows. Charlie nodded to him.

"Let us sing," Reverend Bowers said, and led out in "Bringing in the Sheaves." That's when Barbara noticed that none of the Indians wore gaudy war paint and carried no arms. Slowly she unclenched her fingers.

One of the chiefs came to the door and began to gesture with his hands, touching his mouth and making chomping noises.

Charlie nodded again. To Barbara he muttered, "They're Sioux. I think they're hungry. What can we give them to eat?"

Wildly she looked around. Her glance lit upon the loaves of bread she had baked to feed the guests after the service.

Drawing a weak breath, she moistened her dry lips. "In . . . in that basket is the bread I baked for the after-service meal. That's all I have . . ."

"Go, bring it here."

The room was dead quiet, and the little congregation seemed to focus on her. With shaking legs, Barbara moved across the room and reached for the basket she had placed on the shelf, covered with a clean white cloth.

Charlie took the basket and stepped outside. He handed a piece of bread, already spread with butter, to the Sioux chief who grabbed it greedily and began to wolf it down. The others pushed back their slices and pointed to the butter and shook their heads. What was wrong?

"I don't think they like the salted butter," Pete Parker said to Barbara in a low voice. "What else you got?"

Barbara looked at Charlie. He pointed to a jar of Aggie's raspberry jam. Mame Probst immediately grabbed a knife, pushed her way toward the door and began to scrape away the butter. She spread each slice generously with jam.

"If it's half as good as my wild grape jam, they'll fight over it," she grunted.

"Heap good!" one of the braves exclaimed gobbling up the entire slice. "Running Fox eat."

Silently and stolidly they filed away after the last crumb had vanished. It was a subdued crowd that ate Mame's rabbit stew, Eva Mae's baked potatoes and Ann's greens after the service.

Willie seemed more interested about the Sioux' visit than anyone. "They're the Injuns who's been camped by the crick for weeks now," he said.

After the service he and Henry helped Charlie move the table back indoors after storing the benches in the shed for the next service.

"They hunt . . . they fish," Henry muttered. "Crick is dry now and no fish. Sioux get hungry, so they come for food."

"But we have little food ourselves," Barbara wailed. "I can't be baking for the whole tribe!"

"Look, Barbara," Charlie pointed out, "Our corn is growing well, and we'll have plenty. Why not share if they come again?"

"What if they begin helping themselves?"

"We'll just have to trust God to leave something for us!"

"If you treat an Injun good, he'll be your friend forever," Mame observed sagely. "That's what we learned from the Cheyennes in Okalahomy Territory."

Barbara knew more and more hostile bands were swarming over the western part of Kansas. Things were still peaceful along the Trail, however, since the forts were there.

She remembered the Kaws that had roamed around Marion Centre, especially White Turkey and his kindness to her. Was she actually to become friends with the Indians? Then she chided herself. Hadn't Jesus died for their sins, too? Missionary Mahlon Stubbs at the Kaw reservation near Council Grove strongly believed it. In fact, he had led a number of braves to faith in Jesus Christ. If only Henry Probst had taken a stand for the Lord!

In the weeks that followed, Willie spent every spare minute he could snatch from work to visit the Sioux camp.

"They're teachin' me to ride their ponies, and Runnin' Fox is showin' me how to shoot with a bow and arrow!"

"As long as you don't get one of those arrows in your back," Barbara retorted under her breath. But the whole idea still frightened and bothered her.

Now and then an Indian came to the soddy and begged for food during the next week. They seemed kind, and Barbara gave them whatever she had on hand. Although she didn't fear them as she once had, she was pleased at the way one little squaw gobbled up her fresh cinnamon rolls. Was this why the black eyes grew soft when she pattered to the cabin door and thrust a pair of dainty beaded moccasins into Barbara's hands the following day?

Maybe Mame was right, again. If one showed kindness to an Indian, one had made a friend.

CHAPTER 14

One early morning in mid-July Barbara rode home across the plains from the Pete Parker claim. The ride from the Parker cabin was only two miles across the flat terrain and she should've been enchanted with the scene. All the wheat was cut, tied, shocked and threshed. The four long, tedious steps had yielded an exceptional harvest. The pastures were embroidered with brown and yellow ox-eye daisies fringed in fuzzy, pale-green leaves and wild pinks dotted the scene.

She inhaled her breath sharply, then sighed as she urged her horse onward. Pete had ridden up furiously the night before asking Barbara to come and help deliver Eva Mae's baby. She had been aghast because she'd never witnessed a birthing before. What did she know about delivering a newborn?

"You need Mame Probst," she remonstrated, but Pete had protested, "There ain't time! We gotta get back to the claim—quick!"

The ordeal had lasted most of the night, and not until early morning did the newest little Parker make its arrival, whimpering feebly. Pete seemed to know exactly what to do, and all Barbara had done was boil water, keep Eva Mae's brow cool with damp cloths, hold her hand and murmur soothing words of cheer.

The baby was as black-haired as his father. After Barbara had sponged and oiled the tiny child, she had laid him beside his mother, where he nuzzled at her breast.

Barbara thought Pete looked worried, and his frown deepened. Was the baby all right? The child's whimper was so feeble.

"Thank you, Barbara, for coming to be with us," Eva Mae had cut in wearily. "We'll manage now. Pete knows what to do. But it was so good to have you here."

"Mame Probst would've been much more help," Barbara told her. "I wasn't much help I'm afraid."

"Oh, but you were. You're young and I needed you beside me. You're such a comfort!" But before Barbara had started for home, the baby had given a few weak gasps and lay still.

Barbara rode toward the little soddy now with the dew still sparkling on the grass. She recalled Eva Mae's agonizing cries during the long hours of labor in the hot, tiny shack. She wondered why women had to suffer pain to bring a child into the world and why some newborns are relinquished to death after such an ordeal, especially where little medical help was available. She realized that romance and love were in a dream world, but having babies was part of the real world.

When she rode up to the cabin and tied Queen to the hitching post, Charlie came out to meet her, his hair tousled and black curls tumbling over his forehead.

"Barbara, are you all right?" he asked, taking her arm and leading her into the house. "You look absolutely worn out."

She smiled wanly. "I'm so tired, I could sleep all day. But you and Willie need breakfast—"

"We've already eaten, and Willie's in the barn." He led her to the table. "Here. I'll dish up some mush for you and after you've eaten, you'll go to bed. How did it go?"

Barbara sat down at the table and stared at the food on her plate. Somehow she wasn't hungry. Witnessing a baby's birth had been a trying experience and had unnerved her more than she dared admit. Then to watch it die devastated her completely.

"Pete and Eva Mae have . . . had . . . another boy," she said listlessly. "It was a long night and everything was fine, at first. But—"

"But what, darling?" Charlie prodded as he poured coffee into her cup.

She shook her head. "Baby Paul lived only an hour. Everything's . . . so hard. This lonely country is no place to bring up a family! It's tough enough to face the everyday world, then to deal with life and death and everything else." She stirred her mush idly with her fork.

Charlie didn't say anything. *Now I've hurt him,* she thought.

"I'm sorry," she continued, "but I guess it was a new experience for me . . . to watch that tiny child come into this world, then leave so suddenly. Maybe someday things will be different."

She nibbled at her food.

"Yes. They will be, I promise."

At Mogie's sudden bark, Willie pushed his way into the kitchen. He hung up his hat on the nail behind the door and came toward the table. Barbara noticed the strained look on his usually merry face. Something was wrong.

"Willie, what's the matter?"

He drew a deep breath. "I was just lettin' the cows into the corral when Henry Probst rode up. It seems . . . it seems that the little McNeer girl got bit by a rattler. She . . . she died last night. There'll be a buryin' as soon as they can find a suitable spot. Since there's no graveyard—"

"I'll donate the five acres of land on the southeast corner of our claim for a 'God's Acre'," Charlie announced. "There's a little elm tree for shelter from the sun and we do need a cemetery." He turned to kiss Barbara, grabbed his hat and headed toward the door. "I'll ride to the McNeers and Parkers right away," he shouted. Then he jumped on Queen's back and was gone.

Wearily Barbara started for the bedroom. "I need a nap, Willie," she said in a tired voice. "I've been up all night."

"Sure, Barbara. Go ahead." Willie packed up the dirty plate and carried it to the dishpan. "You sleep as long as you like."

Unpinning her droopy bun, Barbara lay down on the bed. Charlie had already pulled the covers back neatly. She closed her eyes, willing them to sleep. But sleep refused to come. Birth and death had come so swiftly this past night. It was all a part of life, of God's plan, she knew. But it seemed to overwhelm her suddenly, and she wasn't sure how to cope with it. As she lay on the bed, a dizzy jumble of thoughts whirled through her mind. She knew Charlie, as the leader of the small, spiritual flock, would help prepare the children for burial, and she ought to stand by him. Yet, how could she? She wasn't fit to be his helpmate.

An hour later she got up and combed her hair, tucking the feathery tendrils behind her ears, and went about her work.

That afternoon a handful of settlers gathered at the two freshly dug graves in the new little graveyard to lay little Paul Parker and Nellie McNeer to rest. The day had grown unseasonably hot and humid, and Barbara pulled her sunbonnet over her neck, seeking the meager shade from the little elm. She saw Mame and Henry in the background with Ed and Ann Evans beside them. There were a few others she didn't recognize.

As Charlie opened the little girl's homemade casket, Barbara gasped. Nellie, only seven years old, looked like a fragile flower in her pale pink smocked lawn dress. Her long blond hair lay loosely over her shoulders and a perky pink bow above her left ear made her look like a wild rose. Over her breast lay a bunch of red prairie lilies.

Barbara turned away and stifled a sob. How could a vicious prairie rattler take the life of such a beautiful child? It wasn't fair!

Pete Parker stood quietly alone, his handsome face solemn and drawn. Mrs. McNeer sobbed softly as Charlie fastened down the lid of Nellie's crude box. Darren McNeer drew his wife tenderly into his arms and they stood forlorn and sorrowful as Charlie spoke a few words of comfort. " 'Suffer little children to come unto me,' said Jesus, 'and forbid them not: for of such is the kingdom of God.'

"We commit these dear children to You, O God . . . dust to dust . . . ashes to ashes."

Barbara turned away. She couldn't bear to watch as shovelfuls of clods thudded on the crude coffins. *What can I say to Sarah McNeer? To Eva Mae?* she thought. She couldn't think of any words of comfort when she needed them herself.

Impulsively Willie dropped a single rose on Nellie's clodded mound as the McNeers turned away. Barbara recognized it as the lone bloom from the rosebush Aunt Prudy have given her. It didn't matter. The rosebush would remind her forever of little Nellie McNeer. If only there'd been another one for Paul Parker.

As Pete Parker got on his horse, the McNeers climbed into their wagon and drove away slowly. Barbara waited until Charlie and Henry Probst had tidied up the two graves. Mame ambled toward Barbara and placed her bulky arms around the quaking shoulders.

"My, ain't it sad? They say the child never knowed what hit her. And Eva Mae. Well, when you have young'uns, you must trust the good Lord to give you grace to give 'em up, if He wills."

Barbara didn't answer. She decided she would never go through any of this. Taking Charlie's arm, she walked slowly with him back to the soddy. *I'll never be the same again,* she thought.

That night when the stars came out and winked in the black velvet sky, Barbara sat idly on the stoop. The dense, boundless blackness was broken only by the chirr of crickets and swish of prairie grass. Then she saw the cowslip prairie moon swing its cheery way above the sheds. Charlie came out of the shadows and sat beside her.

"I know you've had a hard day, my darling," he said huskily. "First, helping deliver the Parker baby . . . and then seeing it die . . . then the McNeer child laid to rest. But that's all part of being a family. Life and death is in God's plan. You know that!"

She shook her head fiercely. "No, Charlie. I won't have it,

none of it! I don't want a family. First, they come into this world in such pain and agony. And then this wild country snatches them away. So many babies die . . . or children get sick. Women have babies . . . and there's no doctor within miles."

Charlie covered her small hand with his big palm. She saw the sadness in his summer-blue eyes. When he spoke, his voice was firm.

"Barbara, I'd hoped for a family of boys, and maybe a girl or two to help you. If we want to make a go of this ranch, we need a family. We'll manage with God's help. One of these days Willie will be old enough to file his own claim and won't be with us forever!"

Barbara cried big, heaving sobs that didn't want to stop. She jerked her hand away. She couldn't accept the idea of raising a family on the lonely plains. It overwhelmed her completely.

"I hope God doesn't give us any children," she blurted bitterly. "I can't stand to go through birth or death. It just isn't fair!"

In bed that night, she drew away from Charlie for the first time since their marriage nearly a year ago. *If only I didn't love him so,* she cried to herself, beating her fists fiercely into her pillow.

In the days that followed, the prairies were lost in undulating heat that blurred the horizon. Waves of hot air poured from the earth and dust devils were everywhere, scurrying, leaping and blowing across the shadowless land. The leaves of corn shriveled and curled, and it seemed God had forgotten them. Nothing lived . . . nothing breathed. Life dragged on.

Then one day a letter came from Aunt Prudy with news that Vange was in a "family way," and she was eagerly looking forward to a grandchild again, and perhaps a visit to see Vange and Barry. Barbara read the cryptic writing carefully.

". . . I wondered if maybe you and Charlie would have
a child. It would make me a gramma, cause you're
like my child, Barbara. Children is a heritage from the

Lord says the Bible. That makes them speshul.
We may be travlin by way of the Trail if we make the
trip and wood like to see all of you."

Barbara laid the letter down on the table. *Children? A heritage from the Lord? But why would He take them away?* she wondered. Still, He gave and He took away. Blessed be His name. The idea startled Barbara. This God-forsaken land was no place to bring up a family. She wasn't ready to risk it. It took every ounce of faith she could muster to believe that God was in control.

CHAPTER 15

$\mathcal{T}$he long, hot days dragged into late July. Charlie's rows of corn shriveled in the scorching sun. Barbara carried bucketfuls of water to the garden to save it from withering and turning brown.

Willie had helped her pick beans and peas. In spite of the blistering heat, Barbara bent over the little stove as she canned row upon row of vegetables for next winter's food supply.

Willie recalled some of the things his mother did when she was putting up food for winter.

"I remember my Ma boiled the jars in hot water for a couple of hours to make sure the peas would keep," he told her when she didn't know how to process them.

"Did you ever help Aggie and the others dry corn?"

"Corn?" Barbara shook her head. "Oh, I know they cut the kernels off the ears while they were still fresh and milky, but all I did was cut myself!" She stared at her rough, work-worn hands, once pretty and soft.

Willie shook his head. "I guess ya didn't learn how to dry corn then. Well, we'd spread a batch on the henhouse roof and cover 'em with flour sacks for a couple of days." Immediately he started toward the door for a corn knife and some gunny sacks.

"But aren't the kernels too hard by now?" she parried.

He turned. "Maybe some are. But they get drier yet when the sun blazes on 'em." He grinned, grabbed his straw hat and hurried out into the hot sun.

Charlie was cutting a new crop of hay for fodder when he wasn't breaking sod. The sod was a tough thick mass of roots topped by tall, thick grass. No wonder it made sturdy sod-house walls.

Indians were seen everywhere, often riding along the old buffalo trail that cut through the north edge of their claim. Now and then they came to the soddy. A few were friendly, but some were surly and cross. All wanted food and Barbara gave them what they wanted. When an Indian pointed to a loaf of freshly baked bread and grunted, Barbara was afraid to refuse him. Mogie barked shrilly as they shuffled to the door, so Willie kept the dog chained near the house.

Two hours after preparing the corn, Barbara took the last panful of kernels from the table and started for the door so Willie could spread them out to dry. Suddenly the sunshine was gone.

"I do believe it's going to storm this evening," she told Willie who was scooping up the last of the cobs to carry to the hog pen. "We really need a good rain."

Great black clouds were boiling up in the south, obscuring the sun. Somehow they didn't look like rain clouds. Then with a sick feeling Barbara knew why.

Charlie rushed up with the team, dragging the plow behind him. "Prairie fire!" he yelled. "Fill the tubs with water and soak all the gunny sacks you can find. Hurry!"

Barbara looked up briefly. Thick black smoke swirled into the brassy blue sky. Willie grabbed two tubs and headed toward the well. Bewildered, Barbara followed him. Already Charlie had begun to plow a furrow as a fire guard around the buildings. The sky was black now, as though the sun had already set.

Plowing a long furrow west and south of the house, he shouted again, "Hurry! Hurry! Get those wet sacks here!"

As Barbara and Charlie scurried to the well, rabbits bounded out of their way in the tall grass. Quickly filling the tub, Barbara helped him carry it toward the house, soaking the sacks and panting as they worked.

A giant jackrabbit leaped right over the tub just as Charlie grabbed the vat and staggered toward the furrow. Barbara could already see the red flames under the rolling swell of smoke and she shivered in the heat at the awesome sight.

Willie paused to help Charlie start a back fire with the wind shrieking in their ears. Hundreds of birds flew before the fire, and hordes of rabbits bounded in every direction. Snakes slithered through the grass and prairie chickens pattered silently, their necks outstretched and their wings spread.

The backfire was all around the house now as Charlie and Willie beat out the flames with the wet sacks. When it jumped across the furrow, they stomped it out with their feet. Barbara, next to the cabin, was fascinated as the fire roared and hissed in the howling wind. Fear clutched her as twists of flame broke loose and whisked away toward the side of the house. She wrung her hands, wanting to do something but not knowing what.

Pray . . . you can pray. The words beat a hollow tattoo in her bewildered mind. "God . . . our claim." Her voice shook. "Our little claim, Lord, please don't let it burn! It would break Charlie's heart if we lost it. I know I hate the loneliness, the vast emptiness, but . . . oh, I don't want anything to happen to our home. And the tree and two little graves in God's Acre. Oh, Lord, spare them!"

Her eyes, nose and throat stung from the smoke and she brushed her hand over her face to wipe it away. Tears cut smudgy paths down her sooty cheeks and dripped on her once-blue gingham.

Mogie howled. The team was whinnying in high-pitched screams and jerking the rope at the hitching post where Charlie had tied them.

The little back fire moved slowly, crawling to meet the furious big fire. Tumbleweeds, borne by the wind, rolled through the flames and touched off unburnt patches of grass around the sodhouse. The wind rose to a high, crackling shriek as the flames leaped into the air. Charlie and Willie beat furiously around the edges with their sacks, their faces black with soot and smoke.

Then it was over. The fire roared past, and swept down the slope. Charlie and Willie were still beating out the little fires here and there in the yard. One by one the flames sputtered and died.

Willie dropped his wet sack and plodded toward Barbara. "You all right? The back fire . . . saved us," he panted and she nodded as she stumbled back to help Charlie.

"I . . . I prayed," she called out to him.

"I figured you would," he called back.

The air smelled like burnt toast. The prairie spread its naked blackness before them with threads of smoke rising here and there from the smoldering sod as ashes blew in the wind.

When Charlie came toward her, she barely recognized him. His face was caked with smoke and soot. Regardless of his grim appearance, he took her in his arms and hugged her tightly.

"Oh, Barbara, my darling! We almost lost our place . . . but we didn't. Thank God!"

She laid her smudged cheek against his filthy shoulder. "The . . . your backfire saved us, and God heard our prayers," she whispered. "I'm so glad!"

"I'm glad too, Barbara. He promised that, you know, if we trusted Him."

Just then the sound of drumbeats echoed from the direction of the Sioux camp and she tensed. Here and there a rabbit hopped gingerly across the naked black earth and the meadow larks took up their interrupted singing along the scorched fence rows.

As Barbara carried out a pan of water and clean towels, Willie began to scrub the grime from his face.

Just then Henry Probst rode up and pulled to a stop before the soddy. His craggy German face was grimy with smoke.

"Joost wanted to see if you be safe," he muttered, doffing his battered felt hat.

"We're fine. You and Mame all right?" Charlie asked.

"Is all goot. Our dugout is fine, too."

"Wonder if maybe them cantankerous Injuns started the fire to drive us settlers out," Willie muttered.

Henry shook his smoky face. "I t'ink not. They're getting ready for their big buffalo hunt," Henry went on. "That is goot. It sure is on their minds now since so much game ran from the fire."

The smoky haze had slowly lifted from the air, and twilight fell soft and purple over the landscape. In the distance, the Indian drumbeats continued.

"Sounds like they're finally leavin' us, and Barbara's good cookin'," Willie chortled.

Barbara smiled as she went into the sodhouse for more water and towels. As she came back outside, she gazed all around her. Everything was black and grim except for the lone elm tree that shaded the two tiny graves. Her gaze rested on the still-living tree standing against the stark landscape and something deep inside of her made her think of God's mercy. He had answered her prayers again as He had done so many times before.

CHAPTER 16

*T*he blackened prairies began to show tufts of green when the late July rains fell. For several days they lashed from leaden-gray skies across the horizon. Rivers ran down the roof of the soddy and splashed against the window panes in fury. Barbara peered through the rain-mottled glass at the black outdoors until there was only a whisper now and then. When it died down, Willie took off his shoes and rolled up his trousers to go after the cows.

As soon as the prairies dried, Charlie and Willie mended fences and searched for fuel. The few remaining buffalo chips had been charred into sullen ashes. Along Walnut Creek, a line of scrubby trees had escaped the path of the fire. By carefully searching, chopping and cutting, the small heap of firewood slowly grew. Because the fire had wiped out the corn crop, no cornstalks were left for kindling. If the hay grew tall enough, they could always prepare twists for fuel to use in a pinch, Charlie had said.

One day when Willie rode in from Fort Larned, he tossed a letter in Barbara's lap. She had finished another pile of mending and laid it on the table. The aroma of new sweet potatoes simmering in butter-cream sauce filled the damp kitchen.

"You got a letter from Georgia," he said, grabbing a wriggling Mogie in his arms. "Guess somebody there knows where you're at."

"Georgia?" she echoed, tearing open the flap and glancing at the signature. "Oh, it's from Barrister Cornwall. Now what could he—"

"Read it and see."

After hastily scanning the contents she gave a squeal. "Oh, Willie! I didn't know! Oh, where's Charlie? I must tell him."

"Tell him what? That your plantation has mirac'lessly come back to life?"

"Almost. Charlie!" she shouted as she rushed outdoors waving the letter in her hand. "Guess what news I got!"

Charlie had just hung up a freshly mended harness in the barn. He stopped abruptly when she came toward him with the letter in her hand.

"Bad news or good news?"

Barbara smiled wryly. "Both, I guess. This letter comes from John Cornwall, a lawyer in Atlanta. I've heard my uncle mention his name. Uncle Alex took me in for awhile after my mother died. He was my father's brother who died in the war before I came to Kansas."

"Well, what does it say?" Willie dropped Mogie and pulled at her sleeve.

"It says that his lawyer has been trying to reach me, because Uncle Alex Temple left his property to me. I'm the only living heir, it seems."

Charlie jerked his head so quickly that the dark curls tumbled over his forehead.

"That's . . . that's great, darling. And you didn't know you were an heiress?"

"Oh, it's not that simple, Charlie. I'm supposed to go to Atlanta and claim it, in person. But there's no way . . . "

"Somehow we'll make a way, Barbara, if you want to go."

"But, Charlie, I could never leave! Not alone. And you can't get away, can you?"

"We'll pray about it and leave it in God's hands."

She nodded. "Of course. That . . . that's what we'll do." It had never occurred to her that anyone had anything of value left after the war. She hardly knew her Uncle Alex, as she'd only lived with him a few weeks before he went to fight in the Rebel army.

Charlie took the letter in his hands and read it carefully. "Look, darling, did you see this? Cornwall says your expenses will be paid if you come. I think you should go."

Barbara shook her head fiercely. "But I can't go alone! Besides, what would I do with land a thousand miles from here?"

"You could always sell it."

Before she could respond, the rumble of wagon wheels on the lane diverted their attention toward the east as they strained their eyes to see who it was. Then, like a lazy river suddenly pouring over a waterfall, her emotions began to bubble and churn as she exclaimed, "Oh, Charlie . . . I think we've got company. It looks like Uncle Daniel . . . and Aunt Prudy!"

In a few moments it became apparent she was right. As she called out, "Uncle Daniel! Aunt Prudy!" they waved back. After the wagon jerked to a stop, the next few minutes were a maze of hugs and cries of joy. Tears spilled down Barbara's cheeks when she realized how much she had missed her family.

"What about me?" A voice squeaked from among the jumble of trunks and boxes as a bedraggled Bitsy hopped to the ground.

"Bitsy!" Barbara squealed, hugging Bitsy so tightly that her cousin made a funny face as if to show she was squeezed to the bursting point.

"Hey! You're not going to strangle me before I have a chance to look at you, are you?"

After the happy greetings finally ended and she caught her breath, Barbara stood back and stared.

"What . . . what brings you here? I mean, I never—"

"We've just come from Denver, visiting Vange and Barry *and* their new baby daughter, Angela. And she's an angel!"

"Vange? Baby? Where's Aggie? Where's Josh?" she cried still

bubbling from the surprise visit.

"Aggie stayed to help Vange, of course," Bitsy said. "Who else can keep things running smoothly when there's a wedding or a baby or stuff like that? You know Aggie. She knows all about diapering and cooing even though she's never had a young'un of her own. As for Josh, he stayed home to hold down the homestead.

"Barry had sent tickets last month to come on the Butterfield Overland Despatch. We decided to come and see you, too, so we rented this rig at Ellsworth and here we are!"

Charlie had begun to unload the wagon, and after catching her breath, Barbara remembered her manners and shooed the Moores into the tiny house to eat.

Bitsy exclaimed with delight as she stepped across the threshold. "Barbara, you've got a really classy little place here, you know?"

"If it's classy, it's 'cause it's also the schoolroom," Willie quipped and he and Bitsy burst into laughter.

"Well, of course!" Barbara paused, trying to think what to fix for their meal besides the sweet potatoes.

Before long, Uncle Daniel followed Charlie and Willie out to the barn to stable the horses. Aunt Prudy had already picked up Barbara's apron and tied it around her tiny middle.

"Now what's to eat? We're almost starved. They don't feed you so good on the B.O.D."

"You mean you actually came all the way over the Smoky Hill Trail? On the Butterfield Overland? How about Indians? They've been really nasty since spring. The Sioux left their camp along Walnut Creek after the prairie fire only two weeks ago."

Bitsy chortled, "Oh, we played hide-and-seek with a band of Kiowas for awhile. But a calvary troop came along and chased them off. You're lucky Fort Zarah and Fort Larned are so close, although I hear the hostile bands don't always keep their distance."

"That's true. The Sioux left after the prairie fire chased off the game," Willie said.

Barbara had already unwrapped the last slab of bacon and was slicing it in thick wedges for frying. A few prairie chickens or rabbits would've been tastier. There was dried corn boiled with butter to complete the menu.

As the family crowded around the small table later, Barbara was nervous about the first meal in her home for her kinfolks.

"I feel I should apologize," she said after Uncle Daniel had asked the blessing. "You're used to Aggie's cooking, and I—"

"We'll be fine," Uncle Daniel cut in with a nod. "You've learned from Aggie and it shows." His deep-blue eyes twinkled as he scooped up a generous helping of sweet potatoes.

Already Barbara was thinking about where everyone was to sleep. Of course, Aunt Prudy and Uncle Daniel would have the big bed; Barbara and Charlie would make do on the kitchen floor.

"You can have my bunk," Willie offered Bitsy. "I'll take a blanket and sleep under the stars, with Mogie. It ain't the first time."

Bitsy glanced at Willie's bunk on the north wall of the kitchen. "It's not as roomy as my ol' bed up in the loft, Barbie. But I'll sleep fine. I can always lie down on the edge so that I'll soon drop off."

Barbara laughed. *I'm getting as bad as my cousins,* she told herself. *They always laugh at every little thing.* She hadn't been so happy in weeks. Conversation switched from news of Vange and her new baby to the latest happenings at Marion Centre, to Mame and Henry Probst, to the prairie fire and the newest settlers. The afternoon passed quickly in conversation that covered the news from the long stretch of time since they had all been together.

At a lull in the conversation, Uncle Daniel cleared his throat and pushed back his chair.

"Barbara, Charlie tells me you have heard from your Uncle Alex's lawyer at Atlanta about a piece of ground he's left to you."

"Yes. Actually, it's a small cotton plantation." She laid down a fork she was drying. "But there's no way I can go without Charlie."

"If your trip is paid—"

"Yes, it is. But I can't go alone. When I came to Kansas I had no choice but to make the trip alone. But I can't imagine going back there by myself. Besides, what would I do with a parcel of land in Georgia? We live here in the middle of Kansas!"

"Still, it would be a treat for you to go back to your old home. If I were you, I'd take this chance," Uncle Daniel pursued.

"Pa," Bitsy spoke up, "I don't want to leave Ma with the work or I'd offer to go with her."

"Let's see. Rosie could come out to help with the heavy chores if Bitsy went with you," he suggested while spreading a piece of cornbread with blackberry jam.

"But the cost—" Bitsy began.

Uncle Daniel looked up. "God has been good. He has blessed our farming efforts, and we've had some fine crops this summer. I think I could spare the cost of a ticket, if you'd go," he nodded to Bitsy, then continued, "especially since our trip to Denver was free."

"It would be a long, tiring journey," Aunt Prudy put in, "but Barbara has traveled it before. These frontier women learn how to take care of theirselves. I think Bitsy should go with her."

Barbara looked anxiously at Charlie. She couldn't bear to leave her young husband for those long weeks.

He grinned and winked. "Then it's settled. It will do you good to go back to your old stomping grounds. See if it's still intact. Besides, I don't know of anyone I'd rather trust to go with you than your cousin Elizabeth."

"But where would we stay? Hotels are expensive." Barbara wrinkled her forehead.

"Maybe Matthew's mother would keep you. I've picked up several piles of buffalo bones to sell for an emergency. They pay $8 a wagonload to use for fertilizer. You could use some of the money I get from the bones to pay her something, if she'd keep you during your stay."

Barbara frowned. The idea was still so new. Did she really

want to go back? She knew the war had swept across Atlanta and that Yankees had burned the once sprawling city. It wouldn't be the same. And probably most of the people she had known were gone. According to the papers, Atlanta was being rebuilt. If she could see Mammy Crissy and Mammy Louisy . . . but would they still be there? It just couldn't be like it had once been. And yet, if she could sell the land, they would have money to expand their claim and make life easier. Perhaps they could invest in land for Willie, too.

She glanced at Bitsy. "If you'll go with me . . . I . . . I'll go. But it won't be an easy trip, you know."

"Oh, Barbie!" Bitsy cried. "We'll make it. We'll attend balls and pretend we're Kansas aristocrats, not backwoodsy Yankees!"

Barbara's face fell. "With my tattered dresses? I don't see—"

"Don't worry. Cousin Bedelia still sends us her box of hand-me-downs from Ohio each year. We'll salvage something for you." Aunt Prudy added. "We'll make do."

"We plan to take the Santa Fe stage from Fort Zarah to Cottonwood Crossing on Tuesday. Barbie, you can go back with us and stay a few days while we pack and plan. It'll work out fine, I promise!" Bitsy's voice was eager.

Barbara slept little that night. Did she really want to go so far away? Things there wouldn't be the same. Yet if the money from the sale of the property could help Charlie, she had to take that chance. And if Bitsy went along with her for company she wouldn't have to go alone. No doubt Widow Potter could use the money for their board. They'd return as soon as possible after she saw the lawyer.

There was much to do, and think about, and plan before they left. She'd look through her meager wardrobe and wash and iron what was wearable. Her blue traveling suit had been folded away in the trunk for so long. She'd never worn it much since she came to Kansas. With Bitsy, the journey wouldn't be dull. But the thought of leaving Charlie and Willie to fend for themselves bothered her. Yet she knew they'd managed at Marion Centre and probably wouldn't miss her as much as she'd miss them.

Squaring her shoulders, Barbara determined to do her best. With the Moore family's help, the next few days seemed to fly by. It was good to hear Uncle Daniel's booming voice that Sunday as he prayed for special grace for the two young women. Dr. Sternberg had come out to preach, and his messages somehow inspired hope and faith. With Mame and Henry, the Petersons and McNeers, the cabin was crowded even more than usual.

When Mame Probst heard about Barbara's planned trip, she wrapped her big bulky arms around her.

"Now, now, you jes' go have yourself a nice time, Barbr'a honey. Henry an' me will see that Charlie don't get too lonesome. Mebbe when my niece Nance Drubeck from Ellsworth comes around she kin help Charlie and Willie. You don't mind, do you?" she said brusquely.

Barbara laughed and pushed her away gently. "I'm sure they'd manage without me or Nance for a few weeks. Besides, I trust Charlie."

Mame planted a wet kiss on Barbara's cheek while Henry took her small hands in his rough ones.

"You haf a goot trip, young lady," he mumbled rather sheepishly. "Don't you worry none."

After they left, Bitsy let out a delicate snort. "I felt like choking that old rubber ball. The idea! Getting her niece up here to keep Charlie company. Who does she think she is? And who is this 'Nance' person?"

Barbara laughed again. "Well, Mame's as gritty as sandpaper and as snappy as a turtle. I've never met Nance, but from what I've heard she's a dance hall girl. Mame says she keeps the soldiers at Fort Harker happy. If you knew Mame Probst as we do, you'd know she's got to 'manage' things to be happy, especially things that aren't her business, including keeping people happy. She probably meant it as a joke."

Bitsy turned away with a scowl. "Some joke. If you didn't trust Charlie—"

"Of course I trust him, and so should you. Now let's get busy with my packing."

Later that evening everyone got settled into temporary sleeping quarters for the night. After Barbara and Charlie arranged their blankets on the floor and blew out the last candle, a hush fell over the sodhouse.

"We didn't even have a chance to pray about all this," Charlie whispered against Barbara's ear that night. "God already had everything worked out. It must be happening like the Bible says, 'Before you call I will answer.' Now all we need to do is to trust Him to bring things to pass as He sees fit."

As He sees fit. The words lingered in Barbara's ears. *I'm still learning to trust,* she reminded herself. *Now, if everything will work out as we've planned.*

CHAPTER 17

$\mathcal{A}$s the stage jolted over the Santa Fe Trail, Barbara leaned back and closed her eyes. Someone would take the team and wagon that Uncle Daniel had rented back to Ellsworth so that they could return to Cottonwood Crossing faster by stage.

They had bid Charlie and Willie goodbye at Fort Zarah. A mingle of excitement and pain seemed to foment as she thought about her goodbyes to Charlie and Willie. Charlie had held her so tenderly, and she would remember his deep kiss for a long time. Willie had smacked her soundly on her cheek, wearing a sheepish grin. *I'll come back as soon as I can,* she promised herself. Maybe six weeks. Two months at the most.

The Concord coach swayed and jounced from side to side. Ruts from recent rains were still deep. Barbara stared through the dusty windows as she had done three years before. Aunt Prudy nodded and Uncle Daniel seemed to drink in the lush landscape with the faraway look in his blue eyes.

"You're so quiet, Barbara," Bitsy said as she jogged her elbow. "You're not having famous last thoughts about going, are you?"

Barbara sighed and shook her head. "Not really. I know Uncle Daniel's right. I must go back and settle this thing. But having lived in Kansas for three years now, I guess I'm a bit confused about my feelings. I'd dreamed so long of going back to Atlanta when the war was over. But now that I'm going, my mind's all jumbled. I . . . I'm not sure how much to trust my feelings. What will I find?"

"Well, forget the feelings and let's plan on some jolly times," Bitsy countered. "Remember, I'm 17, growing old and staid, not meeting many handsome new men. The Billings and Shreve males have their minds made up and they don't include me. For all I know, I might find a nice, unattached ex-Reb. Especially if we'd attend some wing-ding ball."

Barbara laughed. "You're not that desperate, are you? I have no idea what kind of social life we'll find in Atlanta these days. Just don't be too disappointed if it's dull and dead since the war. The opera house could well have burned to the ground. Of course, if Madame Lackerman can still give concerts on her harp, the way she did five years ago—"

"She will, if she's a plucky musician!"

Barbara smiled. *I can see that my journey with Bitsy won't be dull,* she thought. Her cousin's quips and odd bits of humor had always added spice to life.

The time had passed quickly and they were approaching familiar landmarks. Ahead loomed the Cottonwood Crossing station. Fortunately the river was low and the crossing not hazardous. The trip by stage had gone much faster than by covered wagon almost a year ago.

Josh met them when the Overland pulled into the stage shop. Cousin Lank had leased the ranch to someone else so he could run his store in Marion Centre.

Barbara almost gasped with Josh's crushing embrace. He balanced himself expertly on his stump of a leg as he held her away and looked at her.

"Still as pretty and feisty as ever," he said with a wide grin, flipping the bags onto the wagon. "I see marriage agrees with you, and Charlie's been taking care of my favorite cousin. So, you say you're planning a trip to Atlanta? Just so Charlie doesn't worry that you'll stay in the South when you get there."

"That's why I'm going with her," Bitsy chirked with a toss

of her butter-yellow head. "To drag her back by force if she tries. You don't think Charlie would let her run loose back in Rebel country, do you, without me to look after her?"

Barbara stiffened. To her it was no laughing matter. "Bitsy, please remember the States are no longer *divided*. Let's forget this Rebel-Yankee talk," she snapped.

"I'm glad you've forgiven us these past years." For a moment a cold silence hung between them. Then Josh's sober face split into his wide grin. "Forgive me, Cousin, for my lack of tact. But let's get out to the cabin. Just don't be too overwhelmed at the changes."

As the wagon rattled toward Marion Centre, the prairies were bathed in brilliant orange color, and the hot days at the tag end of summer cooled with a soft evening breeze.

When the wagon creaked up the short lane to the Moore homestead, Barbara exclaimed at the sight of the cabin. Uncle Daniel and Josh had added an ell of logs and rock on the south side.

"That's our parlor," Bitsy informed her. "It's where we entertain company and where young swains come a-courtin'. As if the Moores have anyone left to court since you and Vange are gone," she pouted.

"Well, how about Aggie? You're not 'spoke for' either, you just told me," Barbara said with a catch in her throat.

"Oh, my no! Don't tell anyone," Bitsy whispered in her ear, "but I think the real reason Aggie decided to stay in Denver is a rich ol' broken down miner who comes to town every Saturday night. Of course, she'd pummel me if she suspected I guessed! But never mind. She'll never give up our prairies."

Barbara laughed. One never knew when to take Bitsy seriously. She gazed at the original cabin adjacent to the new lumber of the ell. *The dear old place stirs so many memories,* she reminisced.

The next few days flew by as Bitsy and Barbara helped Aunt Prudy wash, starch and press their few dresses to pack in the light trunk and two small reticules. The box from Cousin Bedelia yielded one good apple-green challis with a tiny white collar edged in white ruching for Bitsy. Aunt Prudy adjusted the sleeves that were too full. There was also a little white bonnet lined with pale green.

"This was meant for you, Barbie," Bitsy cooed as she snatched up the bonnet and jammed it over Barbara's dark curls. "Somehow this never looked right on my yellow hair. Made me feel like my head was stuffed in a bowl of cucumbers drizzled in Jersey cream."

They packed small sacks of dried apples and plums, nuts and toasted buns to save buying meals on the journey. The trip would take them down the Missouri River, and then onto the train at St. Louis to the South.

Barbara had only a brief visit with Rosie and John, who brought over a large bag of "chaw-chaws," as John called the crisply baked berry tarts Rosie had made.

"We had to see you, Barbara," Rosie bubbled. "My, you're as pretty as ever."

Rosie looked completely happy in spite of knowing she could never have a child again.

Finally Josh had loaded their belongings in the wagon and they were off to Council Grove. Barbara waved at friends along the street as the wagon lumbered through Marion Centre. There was no time to visit if they were to catch the stage for Westport Landing.

The trail twisted and turned almost exactly as Barbara remembered it when she arrived in 1863. Of course, here and there a settlement had sprung up and fields of cultivated crops were already checkered with green. But the undulating prairie grass still kept rhythm with the inimitable wind.

Council Grove hadn't changed much from the way it was when she had come to Kansas, although it didn't seem as crude and raw . . . somehow.

After days of long, jostling stage rides, the two young women were relieved to see Westport Landing rising gradually from the river's edge.

Dogs barked and crowds cheered as the stage jogged along the street toward the wharf.

The wind had shifted to the east, and dank, muddy smells drifted from the river. Ahead, the trim riverboat, *Arrowsmith*, drowsed in the late afternoon sun.

An overwhelming feeling of apprehension gripped Barbara and she shivered slightly. Was she ready to embark on this venture unknown to her and known only to God?

"Please help me," she prayed softly. "Lord, give me grace and strength for whatever lies ahead on this journey."

CHAPTER 18

When Barbara strolled on the deck of the *Arrowsmith* the next morning, she could hear the swish of water from the quiet, brown river as the day shimmered over the hills. Already the steamboat wheezed and puffed upstream, the thundering stern-wheel thrashing the water into a wake of white foam that trailed behind it.

The low banks of the river were covered with timber, sometimes interlaced with wild grapevines and tangled brush. Often enormous, fallen trees were piled on one another along the shore and great, white herons glided slowly ahead of the boat. Catbirds scolded among the willows and now and then strange, green birds soared overhead.

She turned at a sound behind her. Bitsy, looking pert and fresh in her pink percale with its full, puffed sleeves, bustled up beside her.

"What do you think, Barbie? Is this going to be a good trip?"

"Oh, I don't know," Barbara drew in her breath slowly. "This river is so peaceful and the boat seems sturdy enough. But I wish I could skip the rest of the journey and walk down Atlanta's streets. I'd grab my inheritance money and hurry back!"

"Don't tell me you're lonesome for Charlie already! You've been gone just a few days. It'll be weeks before you see familiar faces again."

"Yes, I know. Still, I don't look forward to those long, empty weeks ahead."

"Don't worry," Bitsy cocked her head. "We're supposed to have some fun. I promised you that, didn't I?"

"Well, with you this trip won't be dull!" Barbara leaned against the rail of the slow-moving craft. She couldn't help but wonder about the next two months, and an apprehensive feeling crept over her. As if . . . as if something lay ahead that was to change her life, both her's and Charlie's. But what it was, she didn't know. *All I can do,* she decided, *is to leave my life in God's hands*.

The few passengers on board mostly kept to themselves. Barbara noticed Captain Tracey walk across the deck, stopping to chat with the passengers. He looked tanned and handsome with his white cap and uniform and Barbara smiled a little. *He seems self-reliant and sure of himself,* she thought. *That's heart-warming*.

"Good morning, ladies," He tipped the white-billed cap and bowed slightly. "Are you enjoying the trip?"

Barbara nodded. "It's been delightful so far. But since we're traveling to Atlanta, I could almost wish for more speed."

"We must stop at Hermann to take on more fuel. This craft burns a lot of wood, you know. Once the railroad reaches Kansas, your travel will go faster. The rails are already being laid, of course."

"What's all this about Hermann? Sounds terribly German," Bitsy muttered.

"It is. Actually, Hermann began as a dream." Captain Tracey twirled his cap in his hands. "Some 35 years ago, a group of Germans living in Philadelphia formed a stock company and purchased over 10,000 acres of land in the Frene Creek Valley, along this Missouri River. The area must have reminded them of the Rhine Valley in Germany. This colony had plans to preserve their language and customs, making it almost a German state within the United States! Isn't that incredible?"

"I suppose there are castles and wineries?" Barbara asked, thinking suddenly of Henry Probst.

"Not castles. Wineries, yes. There were to be no log cabins for these hardy souls. Houses had to be brick, handmade on the spot! The town is nestled in the foothills of the Ozarks, along the Missouri. Many steamboats have been built at Hermann Wharf, and there's quite a bit of freight business along the river. The steamboat industry supports a good many Hermann residents. In fact, the riverfront is strewn with their wrecks. The *Big Hatchie* blew up there in 1845." Captain Tracey replaced his cap and moved on.

Bitsy's eyes danced. "Can you just imagine German sea captains bouncing along the wharf? I'm anxious to see it. Didn't you stop here when you came three years ago?"

"I didn't pay much attention and I don't think we stopped there at all. But I can't figure out why the Germans felt they had to carve out their own place here. Yet, it probably wasn't much different from the way the States had split into two factions only a few years ago," she said.

"Well," said Bitsy, toying with the ties of her bonnet, "keep in mind that we're one Union now."

"And you'll sing *Dixie*, too?" Barbara asked whimsically.

"Oh, sure. I'll even whistle *Dixie*."

The two young women leaned against the rail and watched the river move by silently. A dark smudge of clouds hung over the hills to the west.

That night a sudden whiplash of rain streaked the porthole windows with runners that reflected orange light from the brass cabin lamp. Barbara noticed the captain standing on the deck as he drew deeply from his pipe and a halo of blue smoke swirled around his head.

It wasn't until the next afternoon that the city of Hermann burst into view. Barbara, who was seated on a deck chair writing a letter to Charlie and Willie, laid aside her tablet and looked at the scenery. Most of the upland surrounding the town was hilly and forested. They were to stop and take on more wood for the paddle-wheeler, according to Captain Tracey. This time she'd pay more attention to the German colony.

Suddenly Barbara grew aware of some excitement among the crew members at the far end of the decks. Captain Tracey hurried toward her, his face agitated.

"One of the boilers has a leak, and we must stop overnight," he said. "We urge all passengers to go ashore and look around while the damage is being repaired. Come back on board before dark, as we hope to leave early in the morning."

She picked up her tablet and went in search of Bitsy who was playing with a circle of children on the other side of the deck.

"Did you hear what the captain said?" Barbara called out. "We'll be delayed for awhile."

Bitsy scurried toward her. "Well, we certainly don't want another *Big Hatchie* episode. This gives us a chance to see this town. Shall we go ashore?"

"We might as well," Barbara said with a resigned sigh. This would delay their arrival in Atlanta, and she'd hoped to get there as soon as possible.

Picking up their full skirts, the two young women stepped down the gangplank at the Port of Hermann as soon as the steamboat had stopped.

Fish smells mingled with the tang of wild vegetation that fringed the banks of the river along Kallmeyer Bluff and hung over the warm afternoon air. The town was tucked into an amphitheater at the base of the Ozark Hills. Holding onto Bitsy's hand, Barbara followed some of the other passengers down Schiller and Market Streets. They meandered up and down along the quaint German business places looking at the ornate brick homes and the Strehly House with its kitchen garden and vineyards which had been the site of a German newspaper.

Homes high above Hermann had a sweeping view of the town stretching west of the Missouri. They could see the Stone Hill Winery perched on a hilltop with its underground arched cellars.

"That's the home of the Vallet family," one of the passengers pointed out the tall, red brick house. "They started the brick manufacturing business, along with growing large vineyards." The house towered above some of the other buildings, imposing and graceful.

A brash, young German wearing a perky Tyrolean hat grabbed Bitsy's arm. "It would gif me great pleasure to escort this lovely young lady to Hermannhof. You will never taste such sausages and rich wines anywhere as are served there."

Bitsy jerked away with a snort. "No, thank you. In Kansas we drink pure spring water and sweet potato coffee!"

She grabbed Barbara's arm and hurried her down the street toward the wharf. Barbara panted at Bitsy's firm pull. "I'm . . . all out of . . . breath. Where are we going?"

"Back to the *Arrowsmith*! I've had enough of this . . . this foreign city on its Rhine. Everything here reeks of wine and prestige. We're country folk, you know!"

The hours had sped by and they heard the shrill toot of the steamboat just then. The sun was already lowering in the west and it was time to get back on board. The boiler had apparently been repaired.

Barbara was exhausted when they reached their tiny cabin. Taking some toasted berry tarts from the sack of food, Bitsy tossed one to Barbara and brought in several tin cups of tepid water.

"This will be our supper, Cousin," she said with a brisk shake of her butter-yellow hair. "I know the water's warm and I know you're tired, but what else do we need?"

"Not even a sip of the wine you were offered?" Barbara's eyes twinkled as she stretched out on the narrow bunk with a sigh.

Bitsy's eyes flashed. "I'd trade every wine key in Hermann for one glass of cold water from our spring!"

A day or two later the steamboat docked at St. Louis. The two young women boarded the steam-powered Ohio and Mississippi railroad. As the locomotive began to snort and puff, Bitsy swayed with the movement of the train down the aisle of their coach, full skirts swinging. She found their seats and beckoned to Barbara.

Barbara flopped most unladylike into her seat as the train

lurched ahead and she drew a deep breath. Somehow she felt more tired than ever. She didn't realize how much she missed Charlie and young Willie until she saw a young man with the curly black hair across the aisle from them. Taking off her bonnet she fanned herself. *How will I ever survive this long, tedious journey?* she wondered. It seemed endless. She was glad Bitsy was with her.

They were to change to the Nashville-Kentucky line at Vincennes. So many tracks had been torn up by the soldiers, and this was the only railroad that reached Atlanta from the west. *Had the trip been so long when I had come to Kansas?* She could scarcely remember.

"You tired?" Bitsy turned to her suddenly after gazing out the windows at the view.

Barbara drew a deep breath. "I guess the excitement of leaving, and roaming all over Hermann the other day has worn me out. But I'll be all right, once I'm rested."

"Now don't get sick on me!" Bitsy retorted. "Let's make this a real lark. How long do you s'pose it will take us to reach Atlanta?"

Barbara shrugged her shoulders. "I don't know. Long enough, I'd say. And without a calendar I'm not even sure what day this is!"

"Calendar!" Bitsy chortled. "Barbie, did you know when the first calendar was produced in the 1600s everyone thought its days would be numbered?"

Barbara burst into a peal of laughter, and the young man across the aisle looked at her sharply. His deep-brown eyes seemed to bore straight through her and she turned away quickly.

Bitsy kept up a lively chatter as the miles sped by. The train stopped briefly at Xenia, shrieked and whistled, then chugged on toward Vincennes. She tried to doze, but the rough, bumpy rails made sleep impossible.

When the shrill toots announced their arrival at the Vincennes station, Bitsy jumped to her feet and dragged her to the wooden platform of the drab little depot.

"Come on! You've got to get out and walk around before we board the Nashville-Kentucky, or you'll be stiffer'n a board."

The young man sprang up from behind them and pawed at Barbara's other arm. "There'll be time for a good meal," he said in a gravelly voice. "I noticed you've been chawin' on dried apples an' other vittles. You must be starvin'."

Barbara drew back hastily. "I . . . no, please. Let me go!"

"What's the matter? You scared of a soldier? It's been a good while since I seen a beautiful gurl like you." He jerked her toward a waiting horse-drawn cab.

"No, I said . . . let . . . me . . . go!" Barbara screamed each word louder that the last as she tried to tug her arm free from his grip.

Bitsy whirled around and heaved her reticule toward the curly head and yelled, "Didn't you hear the lady? She said . . . let go!" And she brought down the heavy bag on the man's head. Abruptly he spun around and stumbled down the board walk.

Barbara staggered toward the depot and threw herself into a wooden seat, gasping for breath. Bitsy dropped down beside her.

"Honestly, Barbara, it's a good thing I was here. God knows what could've happened if I hadn't been here to fend him off!"

Barbara's breath came in short gasps. "Thanks . . . Bitsy. I'm glad you were . . . here. I only hope the next train will come soon. I trust the porter has taken care of our bags?"

"Oh, yes. I saw to it that they'll go when we go. You all right, Barbie?"

"I'm fine now." She cocked her head. "Don't I hear the next train pulling in now?"

Bitsy scurried to the door and peered down the tracks. "Yes, here she comes! I'm glad we didn't have to wait long. Time for a meal indeed! If I hadn't had to rescue you from that evil-eyed Reb, we'd never have made it." She glanced around suspiciously. "I hope he got the message that he wasn't welcome."

Barbara was relieved when the Nashville-Kentucky

chugged to a stop with a hiss of steam. They would soon be on the last lap of their journey.

The coach seemed a bit more comfortable than the previous one. Barbara leaned back to munch on more of Rosie's chaw-chaws as the train rumbled across the tracks that spanned the Ohio River.

A warm summer breeze blew through the open coach windows as she watched the Kentucky landscape drift by. Lush green fields from recent rains sent a whiff of pungent bluegrass aroma through the open windows. She knew that the war had touched Kentucky at Bowling Green and other areas around, although little devastation was visible along the tracks.

Then she grew drowsy and slept the long hours away.

Many hours later, after countless toots and stops at towns and villages along the way, the train grunted into familiar territory. Barbara began to recognize places like Dalton and Calhoun, now battered and ravaged from Sherman's raids. Her heart began to grow heavy.

The landscape seemed smudged, as though a large hand had swept over and crushed it almost beyond recognition. Again she wondered what awaited her in her old home after what seemed like a lifetime of being away from Atlanta.

CHAPTER 19

$\mathcal{A}$s the train pulled into Atlanta, Barbara noticed immediately the old depot was gone. It apparently had not been rebuilt following the burning of the city. Cautiously she and Bitsy alighted amid cinders and mud a few yards beyond the blackened ruins which marked the site. Barbara stared at the rutted area around the station for the equipage of some old friend or acquaintance who might give them a lift to Widow Potter's house, but she recognized no one, black or white. Probably few of her old friends owned carriages now. Times were hard and it was difficult to feed and lodge human beings, much less animals. Nearly everyone seemed to be afoot.

She looked all around the street so denuded of familiar landmarks, as if she had never seen it before. To her surprise she noticed several planing mills and foundries back in operation. She knew homes and businesses were already being reconstructed. No wonder they didn't seem familiar. Several new brick buildings, some three stories high, had already emerged from the blackened embers, and the Gas Works was functioning again.

Bitsy stood beside her, looking this way and that. "What do we do now, Barbie? How do we get to Widow Potter's? I feel filthy with soot."

Barbara pressed her lips together and looked around. A few

wagons were loading at the freight area of the railroad yard, with several mud-spattered buggies and rough-looking strangers, but she saw only two carriages. One was closed; the other was open and occupied by a well-dressed woman and a Yankee officer.

She scratched her arm in frustration. "I . . . don't know, Bitsy. I'm trying to think." The sun beat hot upon the ravaged city and her grimy traveling suit was itchy with sweat.

She'd heard that Atlanta had been garrisoned, with the streets full of Yankee soldiers. At first, the sight of the blue-coats startled her. It was hard to remember the war was over and that she was back home. The comparative emptiness around the train station took her back to 1863. She remembered how crowded the space had been with wagons, carriages and ambulances, and noisy with drivers swearing and yelling, people who had called out greetings to friends when she had left. She sighed heavily.

"I . . . guess there's nothing to do but walk."

Immediately Bitsy picked up the two lightest bags and handed them to Barbara. "Here. You take these. I'll take our little trunk. Which way do we go?"

Barbara stared down the street, trying to recall which direction Matthew's mother's modest cottage lay, remembering only that it was near the outskirts of town. The Atlanta Hotel which had been reduced to a shell was being rebuilt. But where the warehouses had once stood, all seemed bare. There were still wide vacant lots and heaps of smudged, broken bricks in a jumble of rubbish and dead weeds. She set her steps toward Peachtree Street. Bitsy trotted beside her like a faithful puppy.

"Oh, there's the Hefner building!" Barbara exclaimed. She heard the sound of hammering and marched toward the pounding noise. Here and there were sidewalks with the same air of rush and bustle as she remembered. But where were the Confederate ambulances, the familiar people? The she recognized another variation in the scene—the many black people milling about, almost aimlessly. She scanned their faces quickly. Was Isaac among them? Or Toby? Surely they'd help carry her bags.

With a shake of her head, she pushed herself forward. She didn't recognize a single face!

They walked slowly down Marietta Street and passed the lot where the Poindexter house had once stood. Only a few jutting rocks from the foundation and the chimney remained, except for a pair of forlorn, stone steps leading to nothing. Could this have been the same place she had once attended a ball, wearing her pale pink taffeta belted with a circle of silver? She gulped at the memory, trying to swallow the lump in her throat. Now and then she paused breathlessly for the walk left them winded.

Here and there it seemed like a thriving city, rapidly rebuilding places of ruin into a hustling, hurrying town. The streets were choked and noisy with shiny carriages of Yankee officers' wives and the newly rich Carpetbaggers who splashed mud as they passed by. Once she had known nearly everyone, but now the strangers depressed her. Obviously Atlanta was again the hub of activity as it had been before its destruction, and she shook her head over the changes.

"Do you s'pose the Widow Potter's place is still here?" Bitsy burst out suddenly after picking up the trunk once more. She pushed back her bonnet from her damp face. "How much farther?"

Barbara jerked her head in exasperation. She looked up and down the street. They had trudged countless blocks for the past hour. Yes, there was the Central Presbyterian Church which had been only a block or so from the widow's house. Most houses here looked intact but shabby.

"I . . . I don't know, Bitsy. But the fire apparently didn't reach this part of the city. We should find her place before long. It's a yellow frame house with a mansard roof, and a cupola over the front entryway."

Most houses looked bedraggled, the gardens and lawns overgrown with weeds, all gone to ruin. But of course, few had money to hire help to keep things neat and trim.

Inhaling a deep breath, Barbara pushed on, her arms aching with the load of the two reticules she was carrying. Sweat beaded her face and trickled down the back of her neck. She heard Bitsy puffing behind her with the "light" trunk that was feeling quite heavy by now.

As Barbara looked up and down the street, she was puzzled. She couldn't find the yellow frame house. Would the widow still be in her home once they found it?

"Oh, God," she whispered, "Please let her still be there!" After coming all this way and not finding her . . . she didn't dare let fear envelop her.

Just ahead she saw a familiar green two-story structure. Miss Lily, one of Mrs. Potter's neighbors had once lived in the apartment. She whirled around quickly. That was it!

"Now I remember! Just past the ugly green house . . ." she panted, "is where she lives."

With a fresh burst of energy the two dragged themselves toward the yellow frame house with its cupola just as Barbara had remembered it. The outside looked rundown with peeling paint, and loose shingles flapped from the mansard roof. It didn't seem possible this was the same neat place where Matthew had lived with his mother.

Barbara paused before turning up the walk of broken stones, then resolutely she marched up the shabby porch.

Setting down one of the bags, she raised her hand and rapped sharply. She turned quickly to see if Bitsy was behind her. The familiar toss of her blond head under its bonnet reassured her, and she grinned weakly.

At the creak of the front door, Barbara took a deep breath.

"Yes?" The woman at the door looked much older than her 44 years. Her face seemed drawn and creased with worry lines, her drooping brown hair twisted into a shapeless bun. Her black dress was clean, but faded and patched.

"Mrs. Potter? It's me, Barbara. May we come in?"

"Barbara Temple? Oh, Barbara! Yes, come in!" She paused to give Barbara a searching glance, her voice a soft drawl. "Why . . . I hardly recognized you. But come in, . . . come in!

As she held open the door, Barbara and Bitsy stepped over the threshold. The familiar cabbage-rose carpet still covered the parlor floor, its colors now faded from wear.

"This is my cousin, Bitsy, . . . Elizabeth Moore," Barbara said as Bitsy followed her inside. "She came with me."

Mrs. Potter nodded in Bitsy's direction and took Barbara's bags and set them on the floor, then placed an arm around her shoulders.

"Let me look at you, child. Why, I hardly recognized you! You're lookin' right pert, except maybe some tired. And somehow you look countrified. Please sit down." She pointed to the shabby armchair and horsehair sofa. "What brings y'all here? You've heard about Matthew, of course." Her face clouded.

"Oh, yes, Mrs. Potter. The government notified me shortly after it . . . happened." Barbara sat down, happy for the chance to rest after the long weary walk. "I'm so sorry, Mrs. Potter. It must have been very hard for you."

"Nobody knows what I've suffered." The widow's voice became a whine. "It's been awful! And what we've been through since the war ended would curl your hair, if you knew!"

"We've seen some of the devastation downtown, Mrs. Potter. It must've been terrible."

Mrs. Potter pulled up a small rocker and sat down on its edge. "The fire, oh, it was horrible! All the area of Peters and Fair Streets is destroyed. And many of the magnificent mansions are gone. And the railroads, the Gawgia depot . . . it's an ocean of ruins! The city from the center to the very edge was one sheet of flame including several fire stations. I escaped only because Miss Lily and I grabbed what we could carry and headed away from the fire. We walked and walked and hid in the woods for a day. Then we came back expectin' to see our homes in a pile of ashes, but somehow parts of the city was spared."

"How awful!" Bitsy whispered.

"Y'all couldn't hear a human voice on the street, no children, no drays, no wagons. No whistles from the railroad yard, no brayin' of mules. Everythin' was hushed in the silence of death. Ruin was everywhere!"

Barbara nodded in sympathy. "It must have been very hard to come back to all this . . . devastation. But Atlanta will never die. I'm glad they're already rebuilding. And many homes are still standing."

"But nearly one out of every three houses was burnt! And all because of those awful Yankees!" the widow snorted.

"Thank God you were one of the lucky ones whose home was spared," Barbara said soothingly.

"Maybe so. But we have nothin' left. I'm practically destitute. What little I have to eat is what I've growed in my garden this summer. With my darkie, Becca, gone, I have to plant and hoe every bit of it myself!" She turned over her rough hands and looked at them. "No thought of all the care I once provided for her. These darkies scooted away as soon's they learnt they were free. So you see, there is no way y'all can stay with me. I hardly have enough for myself. I mostly live on grits."

"Well, Mrs. Potter," Barbara tried to speak cheerfully, "This will change for you. Bitsy and I have come back here because I learned I was to inherit some property from my Uncle Alex Temple, and we want to pay you if you'd allow us to stay here."

The faded eyes brightened. "Oh? Then of course I'll put you up, if y'all help with the work."

"Never fear, Mrs. Potter," Bitsy warbled. "We haven't lived with Aggie Moore's cooking skills for nothing! That's my eldest sister who is a great cook. And Barbara can bake a corn pone almost as good as Aggie's. At least, Charlie hasn't complained."

"Charlie?" Mrs. Potter's eyes widened. "Who is he?"

"Barbie hasn't gotten around to telling you," Bitsy offered. "She and Charlie Warren have been married a year. They live in a sodhouse—"

"Barbara, married? But what about Matthew?" Mrs. Potter sputtered, one hand at her throat.

"Matthew's gone, Mrs. Potter," Barbara said quietly. "Yes, his death hit me hard. But God was very real to me and helped me cope with my grief. Then when Charlie wanted me to marry him, the Lord showed me my marriage to Charlie was His will."

"But, . . . but you and Matthew. I don't see how you could forget my son so soon, and throw him aside for a man you hardly knew. I s'pose he's a Yankee?" she spat out the words.

Barbara shook her head staunchly. "There was nothing to throw aside, Mrs. Potter. Matthew was gone. And there was Charlie, a very special young man, steady and dependable, and his young brother Willie! They lived across the Cottonwood River from Uncle Daniel."

For a long time Mrs. Potter stared unseeing at her worn hands in her lap. She rocked back and forth slowly as though trying to digest this new information. Suddenly she got up.

"Well, then. Y'all must be hungry. I don't rightly know what's to eat—turnips, maybe. With onions on the side. And grits."

Bitsy jumped to her feet. "Let me take over the kitchen, Mrs. Potter. You just sit down and catch Barbie up on all the Atlanta news. We may have a few dried apples left in our sack. I'll check."

Without another word, Bitsy scudded into the roomy kitchen and soon Barbara heard the slamming of pots and flatware.

Barbara turned to Widow Potter who perched on the edge of her rocker once more. "I grew up while I was in Kansas, Mrs. Potter. Before I arrived, I was a spoiled, selfish Southern brat who thought only of herself, and too stubborn to know it!"

"I s'pose you became a Yankee yourself," Mrs. Potter said bitterly, "like your pious Uncle and his peasant family! What utter gall for him to insist y'all go north to the wilds of Kansas!"

"When Uncle Alex joined the army, it was good that they invited me to come and live with them. Where else could I go?" she asked without expecting an answer.

"I'm an American, Mrs. Potter. And this nation is no longer

divided into North and South." Barbara tried to keep her tone gentle and firm. "At first I was fiercely loyal to the South, but Uncle Daniel's family soon showed me through their gracious living that in God's sight there's no difference. That we are all created equal."

The widow gave a little snort. "If you'd seen all those uppity Yankees a-swarmin' over Atlanta's streets after Sherman's raid, you wouldn't have said that! And those good-for-nothin' darkies. They say they're free, and don't need to work. Well, lots of them are starvin' and who feeds them? The city of Atlanta which has little enough food for itself! All you see is soup lines. Darkies standin' in lines for blocks."

Barbara glanced at the kitchen and saw Bitsy beckoning to them. "I think our meal is ready," she broke in. "Shall we eat?" She took Mrs. Potter's arm and led her to the kitchen where Bitsy was taking out a pan full of cornbread from the oven. The aroma of turnips, simmered with onions and spices made her hungry. The once-gay checkered window curtains hung limp on the kitchen windows, dallying faintly in the hot summer breeze.

As they sat at the small, white painted table, Mrs. Potter sniffed and grabbed for the bowl of stew.

"Barbie will say the blessing," Bitsy cut in quickly. "We're most grateful to God to be here."

"Grateful? For what?" Mrs. Potter scoffed. "If you only knew what it's been like. Why! I've been right scandalized. A bunch of congressmen came up with a Civil Rights bill just this year. It declared all persons born in this country to be citizens, mind you . . . including those feckless darkies! They now have votin' privileges, can you imagine that? Those shiftless darkies like my Becca don't know what the word votin' means. And now they're supposed to be equal to us—we, who built this whole Confederacy! They don't know the first thing about workin' for a livin'. Sure, they worked in cotton and tobacco fields, but they don't know how to lay a brick or build a house. So there's a lot of thievin' goin' on too, along with standin' in soup lines."

Barbara shut her ears to the verbal onslaught as the poor

beleaguered woman seethed with bitterness. Was this the gentle, gracious woman who had been such a staunch volunteer in the hospital auxiliary at one time? They finished the meal in comparative silence.

Bitsy began to pick up the dirty plates and carried them to the work table then poured water into the dishpan.

"I didn't know how to fix grits," she grimaced.

Barbara watched her silently, and leaned back in her chair. *I should help with the dishes*, she thought, *but I'm bone tired*. It had been a long, wearying day. Charlie and Willie would be choring the cows and chickens about now, and suddenly Barbara wished with all her heart she was back with them on the lonely plains. Widow Potter's bitter words about Yankees still rasped in her ears.

Mrs. Potter slowly arose from her chair. "I hope y'all don't mind sharin' the spare room—the room that used to be Matthew's. It's not as nice as it once was. I've haven't been able to keep up my house. But if you're as tired as you look—"

"We're grateful you've taken us in, Mrs. Potter," Barbara said again. "Of course, we don't mind sharing a room. We don't want to make things harder for you than necessary."

"Well," the woman tossed her head. "You were almost my daughter once, Barbara. I haven't forgotten that. I only hope your Yankee husband appreciates you!"

Slowly Barbara pulled herself to her feet. With a stiff little smile she replied, "I guess I haven't appreciated Charlie enough." She stifled a yawn, and walked toward Bitsy bending over the dishpan. "Where's the dish towel?"

"All done, Barbie. Let's go to bed. I'm so tired I'm asleep standing up. Where's the bed?"

Picking up her reticule, Barbara wished Mrs. Potter a quick good night and headed toward the neat, square room across the hall. The floor was bare and the once highly polished boards had lost their luster, although the large walnut bed looked inviting with its bright patchwork quilt. She sat down on the edge of the bed and began to unlace her shoes, almost too weary to draw them off.

As she shook out the grimy, blue, traveling suit, she noticed Bitsy ogling herself in the mirror, sticking out her tongue.

"What are you doing, Bitsy Moore?" she asked. "You've been awfully quiet all evening. That's not like you at all."

Bitsy whirled around and made a wry face. "I'm staring at my tongue; I've been biting it off so I wouldn't tell that woman where to get off, the way she's railed us Yankees! I just had to see if my tongue was still all there."

Barbara smiled to herself as she pulled on her thin summer nightgown. *What a typical Bitsy response*, she thought.

Mrs. Potter has no one, she reminded herself with a feeling of guilt. And I have Charlie and Willie and Uncle Daniel's family—and the Lord!

CHAPTER 20

*W*hen Barbara pried her eyes open the next morning, bright August sunshine stabbed the yellow walls of the tiny bedroom. She cocked her head slightly, suddenly remembering she'd spent the first night back in Atlanta after all the years she'd been away. Bitsy's side of the bed was empty. Barbara sat up quickly and began to pull on her clothes.

The sky was rinsed a pale eggshell blue and the scent of magnolias drifted through the open window. A wren twittered in the branches of a mimosa tree, and memories of her childhood on the plantation stirred. How many sweet, bright mornings she had awakened with the sound of birds and the bustle or voices of darkies busy with after-breakfast chores! The aromas of frying ham, grits and fresh johnny-cake with maple syrup had greeted her as she had come down the wide, curving stairway through the hall to the small dining room. Mammy Crissy had hovered over her like a mother bird, coaxing the lazy birdling to "eat hearty."

Now she pulled on the rumpled, faded, green-sprigged delaine and hurried across the hall. Bitsy was bent over the washtub in the kitchen scrubbing their dirty travel clothes. A kettle of grits simmered on the back of the stove and a pan of cornbread sat half-eaten on the worktable.

"Morning, Barbie," Bitsy sang out cheerfully, pausing to

shake out a pair of Barbara's pantaloons before sudsing them in the tub of hot water. "You rested up from our weary wandering?"

Barbara nodded. "I was so fagged out, I slept like a fox in a cottonwood thicket. Why didn't you wake me? It's time I did my share of work around here. Where's Mrs. Potter?"

"In the garden, grubbing out a few carrots for our dinner. Breakfast's on the stove. After you've eaten, you can hang out the clothes. I'll go somewhere to look for a chicken to cook for dinner. It's plain to see the widow hasn't eaten hearty in a long time. She made . . . ugh! . . . grits!"

"It's probably all she had. As soon as I've settled things with the lawyer, we'll head back to Kansas. We don't have funds to stay long."

Bitsy looked up from the tub, her face flushed and damp. "Ready to leave Atlanta so soon when we just got here?"

"Everything's changed. Besides, I want to get back to Charlie. I've missed him and Willie, you know."

"When do you see Mr. Cornwall?"

"He said he'd be at the National Hotel, and will send word."

"Does he know where we are?"

"I wrote to him and told him we hoped to stay with Widow Potter." Barbara paused to fill a plate with grits. "I'm sure they'll find me . . . somewhere. I only hope this won't take long."

She didn't remember the last time she had eaten grits and devoured them greedily.

After she had eaten, she washed her plate in the dishpan and picked up the basket of clean, damp clothes.

She was hanging up the fresh, starched dresses on the line when a voice sounded behind her. As she turned, her eyes lit up. A young, black boy in faded gray pants and a red shirt eyed her sharply.

"You Miss Barb'ra, ain't you?"

"Toby! It's really you?" She threw her arms around him for a warm hug. He drew away quickly. "Oh, Toby, it's been so long!" She moved back and looked at him. "What brings you here?"

"I'se workin' at the Nash'lle Hotel totin' bags and carryin' messages. Masser Cornwall sens dis note for you." He handed her a crumpled envelope, then waited as she opened it and read it aloud.

> "Dear Barbara,
> I will be out of town for the next few days. On Friday,
> Toby will bring you to the National. Perhaps we can
> settle matters quickly.
> Signed,
> Barrister Cornwall"

She frowned a little. "Friday? That's in three days. I'd hoped it would all be settled before then. But I guess I'll have to wait."

Toby turned to leave. "Den I pick you up. Masser Cornwall let me drive his rig. I cum back for you on Friday." And as he started away, Barbara touched his arm.

"Oh, Toby! It's good to see you. I'm glad you have work. What . . . what of the others? Do you know what happened to Mammy Louisy and Mammy Crissy? And Isaac?"

"No'm. We's free now, Miss Barb'ra. We goes where we pleases." He turned on his heel and strode away.

As Barbara hung up the last of the clothes, Bitsy put on her bonnet, grabbed her shabby purse and hurried out the door.

"Wish me luck. I hope this 'hunter' will come back with some grub. Mrs. Potter says there's a market down the street by the park. Farmers bring in whatever produce they can spare, and there might even be chickens."

Barbara went indoors and began to tidy up the kitchen. Mrs. Potter was seated in her usual rocker, her black dress pulled primly over her thin legs.

"I found a few more carrots. If your cousin brings home a hen, we'll have some fixin's for a stew."

"Yes," Barbara said, straightening the shabby cloth that covered the once-fashionable dining table. "We want to make things easier for you."

"But you aren't well-off yourself, are you?"

"We raise our own chickens and livestock for meat, Charlie shoots some rabbits and wild ducks and we put up all the vegetables we can. We actually have plenty to eat."

The widow shook her wispy head. "I never would've believed it, Barbara. You were always so proud once, and never lifted a finger to do anythin' when you were here. But since the war, not many folks in Atlanta can afford help, with the slaves bein' freed. Not even those who were once well-fixed."

"Atlanta will rebuild, I'm sure. Some day things will go better for you too."

"But not until those confounded Yankees leave!" Her gray eyes flashed.

Their conversation was interrupted by Bitsy's slamming through the back door, swinging two squawking hens in one hand and a bag of produce in the other.

"Look what I've got!" she bubbled. "The market had a surplus today and I got these fat broody hens and some yams and sweet corn. We'll have a feast tonight. How long do we stay in Atlanta, Barbie?"

"I'm not sure. I can't see Lawyer Cornwall until Friday, according to the note Toby brought me. He's staying at the new hotel on the corner of Whitehall and Western streets. I understand it's a fancy place," Barbara said, picking up the bag of vegetables and heading for the work table.

As Bitsy took the two hens to the little shed in the rear of the yard, Barbara piled out the firm, fresh ears of corn and sweet potatoes, happy to replenish the widow's meager larder.

"Why didn't you tell us all about the new buildings and things that are going up around here?" Bitsy said standing in front of the widow with an accusing stare.

"Like what?" the woman grumbled.

"Like . . . the new Atlanta Female Institute where all branches of English literature, French and music will be taught. Not to mention the women's magazine, *Ladies Home*, and the new assembly hall and theatre, like Davis Hall. Plus the baseball team that's been competing with other teams. You made it sound as though Atlanta was dying. It's really thriving!"

"Who told you all that?" Mrs. Potter said with a frown.

"I asked a few questions, and I heard from people who were buying goods at the market. There's a lot more you haven't told us!" she snorted.

"Well, with all the nice old homes destroyed, the Yankees, the burglaries, the—"

"In fact, let me tell you something, Mrs. Potter." Bitsy's voice grew saucy. "You know, I talked to Mrs. . . . . Winship, I think she's called. She's giving a fancy ball tonight in her home and she wants us to come."

A look of sadness crept over Mrs. Potter's lined face. "Whatever has possessed her? Did she also tell you that two of her sons were killed by Yankees? She's a member of the Atlanta Memorial Association that's bringin' home Confederate soldiers to be reburied in the new cemetery. It's bein' re-fenced and enlarged. And then to have the gall to give a ball!"

Bitsy drew a long, slow breath. "The point is, Mrs. Potter, these folks aren't looking back, they're moving ahead. Her party is to give the people a pat on the back for what they've done and are doing. I think we should go, don't you?"

"I can't. I don't have a black ball gown."

"Black!" Bitsy scoffed. "Why wear black?"

"My son, Matthew—"

"Your son, Matthew, died way back in '64, and that's long ago. Why are you still in mourning?"

The widow turned away. Barbara almost felt sorry for her. She obviously had nothing to live for outside of her son—a son who would never come back.

"But you and I will go, won't we, Barbie?" Bitsy prodded. "We must get out and meet people. I promised you we'd have a lark. Here's our chance. At least this once!"

Barbara frowned. "All I have to wear that's still a bit stylish is my green bombazine."

"You wouldn't actually go to a ball wearin' somethin' so colorful?" Widow Potter said with a scandalous look.

"Why shouldn't I?" Barbara's blue eyes flashed with sudden

determination. "It was my wedding gown. Charlie, my husband, is alive, and for that I'm very grateful. Bitsy, you're right. We need a bit of fun. I'll help you fix that chicken stew now."

She began to scrape carrots with a vengeance. It had been so long since she'd attended one of Atlanta's balls. Now that the war was over, its people needed some light-hearted activities, although it wouldn't seem like much to her without Charlie.

As she bent over the pan of vegetables, a wave of tiredness swept over her, but she brushed it aside. Of course, she was a respectable married woman, not some flighty wench. But Bitsy had so kindly accompanied her here and needed this "lark" as she called it.

Mrs. Winship had promised their carriage to pick them up according to Bitsy. After the hearty chicken stew, the two young women spent an hour preparing for the ball. Barbara curled and rolled her thick hair at the nape of her neck, and rummaged in her jewelry box for the jade earrings. The green bombazine looked shabby, yet the old flair for style was evident. Bitsy slipped into the apple-green challis, which looked perfect with her yellow curls.

Mrs. Potter's disapproving glance followed them out the door when the Winship carriage arrived.

"Don't get too carried away with partyin'," she said tartly when they left.

Bitsy's giggle followed the widow's dire words as they stepped into the carriage.

The drive was short, and the pale yellow glow from the heavy brass lanterns spilled over the carriages that moved slowly along the drive of the once-proud mansion. The foyer was ablaze with its candle-lit chandelier and soft, enchanting music floated from the band in the large ballroom beyond the double doors. The room was filled with laughter and the steady hum of voices as couples spun around the room.

Barbara and Bitsy paused just inside the door and watched the smooth, dancing couples move over the polished floors. Women looked like proud dolls snipped from colored paper, hoopskirts swirling with shabby ballgowns. They pointed their toes and flirted their bright eyes, spinning round the room like flying peacock feathers. Their chatter in drawled Southern voices was thick as honey.

"Oh, dear!" Bitsy wailed, "And I didn't bring my hoopskirt. In Kansas we don't need fuss and feathers."

The men, a few in gray, tattered uniforms, were remnants of Southern gentry, proud and handsome. The rest were liberally sprinkled with the dark blue of Yankees.

Barbara and Bitsy stood off to one side, taking in the gay scene, waiting to be acknowledged. A young man approached them and laid his gray-sleeved arm on Bitsy's shoulder.

"May I have this dance, Miss?"

Bitsy looked startled, then turned to Barbara. "I . . . I . . . well, really!" She tossed her golden head coquettishly. "I don't care to dance with someone I don't know!"

Barbara turned her head away with a faint smile. *Bitsy's afraid to admit she doesn't know any other dances than folk dances,* she thought.

"We just arrived, and we want to see our old friends first," Barbara offered graciously.

"If I introduce myself, you can call me a friend," the young man returned quietly. "I'm Derek Adamson, one of the lucky ones who came back. Let me tell you about Bull Run . . . "

Barbara left the two in animated conversation. She was sure Bitsy could handle the ex-Reb and tell him all about Josh's loss of leg.

As she wandered around the floor, she headed for a cluster of young women waiting for their partners to bring food and drinks. Suddenly she spotted a familiar face.

"Mollie Crenshaw, am I right?" she burst out eagerly.

The woman stared at Barbara, who wondered for one wild moment if she'd made a mistake. But there was no doubt. She recognized the woman's high cheekbones and tawny hair piled into the same chignon, from Miss Mallory's Academy.

"Ba'bara . . . Temple?" Mollie asked hesitantly. "Is it *really* you? Girls, look heah . . . Ba'bara Temple, no less! Where've y'all been hidin'? Didn't y'all leave for the crude prairie place in Kansas awhile back?"

Barbara hesitated a bit at Mollie's heavy accent, then she smiled. "Why, yes. Yes I did. To live with my Uncle Daniel Moore and his family. Maybe Kansas has been wild in the past, but she's fast becoming settled . . . although not as sophisticated as Atlanta perhaps. It's there I met Charlie—"

"What about Matthew Pottah?" Lou Anne Maxwell cut in. "Weren't you two engaged?"

Barbara nodded. "Yes, but he was killed, you know. And then I met Charlie . . . "

Barbara's evening moved like a dream. Others, including several silver-haired dowagers, recognized her as the daughter of Colonel and Candace Temple. Although their lifestyles had changed since the war, their gaiety almost made her feel as though she had never left. The glitter of ballgowns, many of them definitely shabby now, stirred deep memories for her, and a sudden longing for the old life in Georgia erupted. If only Charlie were here to enjoy all this with her! It was so different from the simple sodhouse and country cooking, from neighbors like Mame and Henry, and life with Charlie and Willie. Just the gay party of happy people did something to her, and excitement suddenly budded her spine.

Then a wave of dizziness swept over her, and she clutched at the nearest pillar.

"Tell me all about yourself, Barbara," the bejeweled Henrietta Maxwell said graciously. "All about your husband and the . . . the plantation . . . or did you say ranch? . . . where y'all live."

Barbara steadied herself and gulped. "It . . . it's not a ranch in the real sense yet. But some day Charlie and I hope to raise vast herds of cattle."

"And your ranch house? Must be most comf'table and cozy," another woman drawled.

How could she tell these women about the tiny, lonely soddy, the Indian scares, the prairie fires . . . where she felt alone and forsaken, sometimes for weeks?

"I . . . uh, well, it . . . it's not . . . nothing much, really. But some day—"

"You were fortunate to have escaped the horrors of war these past years." Tootie Connington cooed in her low, sweet voice.

"No. No, we didn't escape entirely. My cousin, Josh Moore, fought too. He came home with only one leg. But—"

"Kansas. Isn't that John Brown's hideout? And William Quantrill? They really created a terrible stir. Yankees!" Someone spoke at Barbara's elbow. "Are you one of them, too?"

She felt herself grow dizzy again, and very, very tired. She groped for a response.

"Yes . . . no, yes! But my Uncle Daniel always believed in the Union. He was fiercely loyal to a united nation." *Why do I feel so disembodied, so alone, so afraid? Please help me, Lord!* she prayed silently longing for a steady shoulder to lean on. Then the dizziness passed and she smiled and reveled in the attention she was receiving from the women. *If only Charlie were here,* she thought again, *it would be perfect.*

The dazzling lights, the music, the reunion with old friends swept over her in heady waves. How could she ever go back to the barren prairies, the hard work and loneliness? God suddenly seemed very far away.

She made her way slowly toward Bitsy standing on the north end of the room. Derek Adamson had apparently left, and her cousin stood alone and forlorn staring at the dancers spinning on the polished floor.

"Bitsy? Are you having a good time?" Barbara touched the green challis shoulder.

For a moment a shadow crossed Bitsy's face. "I . . . I thought I was . . . then suddenly all I wanted was to go home, back to Kansas and our enchanted prairies. I've had enough of Atlanta society. I've been stranded here by myself most of the evening. After all, I am a *Yankee*! And they wouldn't let me forget it!"

"But you were the one who was so set on coming."

"I know. And now I'm ready to leave. Shall we ask the Winships to call the carriage?"

The ballroom had grown hot and stifling and the smell of sweat, cigarette fumes, and fine wines made Barbara's head reel. She knew they had to leave before she became ill.

"All right. But I did promise Mrs. Maxwell we'd join her for lunch at the Calhoun House tomorrow, across from the Georgia depot. She was one of Mother's best friends." Barbara hesitated. "She will foot the bill."

The night was cool and dark as they hurried to the wide verandah. Breathing deeply, Barbara's head cleared. Billowing clouds rolled up from the north and a brisk wind rocked the carriage gently back and forth as it clattered down the avenue.

When it stopped before Mrs. Potter's yellow cottage, Barbara steadied herself on Bitsy's arm as they walked to the porch.

"You didn't imbibe, did you, Cousin?" Bitsy said lightly. "You positively wobble."

"You know I don't drink! I guess it was the—the stifling ballroom, the heady atmosphere. I began to feel faint."

A lone candle burned on the mantel when the two came in. Mrs. Potter trotted from her bedroom with a yawn.

"So how was the ball?" she asked, clutching a skimpy robe around her thin figure.

"Almost like old times," Barbara said with a tired laugh, "meeting my friends again. If I hadn't been so tired—"

"I knew it! Y'all never should've left Gawgia," the widow cut in. "You might have lived with me, and we could've mourned Matthew together. You would have been a comfort to me then, just as you're bein' now. And y'all never should've allowed that Yankee Charlie to talk you into marryin' him!"

Barbara shook her head. A comfort to the widow? Right now, she needed the comfort of a bed. She followed Bitsy into the bedroom without a response. *Why did she feel so strange?*

"That woman!" Bitsy snorted. "She'd have made you wear black, too, all these years. And I bet she would like for you to stay even now. Why didn't you tell her off? I'll be horribly glad when we leave."

Shaking her head, Barbara drew off the green bombazine

and loosened her hair. "I didn't want to upset her. But . . . it was good for me to come back. I do know I love Charlie more than ever. I only wish he were here with me right now."

CHAPTER 21

*G*ray rain lashed at the windows when Barbara opened her eyes in the morning and she drew the covers over her head. It reminded her of rainy days on the plantation when darkies tackled indoor jobs, like scrubbing the kitchen ceiling, then applying whitewash. She could almost smell it now, acrid and penetrating.

Then she stirred into full wakefulness. Bitsy was up early as usual. Barbara dressed slowly and made her way to the kitchen. The heady aroma of buckwheat pancakes wafted through the dark, steamy kitchen and she drew in her breath sharply. It was almost as though she saw Mammy Crissy bending over the large, black skillet and flipping the cakes to brown just right.

Bitsy looked up from the stove. "So you're up. You looked so jaded I didn't have the heart to wake you. Widow Potter said she was hungry for buckwheat cakes. How about you? I was glad she didn't ask for grits!"

Barbara's head cleared. "I've almost forgotten how buckwheat cakes taste. I remember how good they were with sausages."

"We'll spoon some molasses over them since we have no sausages, unless Charlie has shot a deer."

"Charlie! What does he have to do with buckwheat cakes in

Atlanta?" Barbara burst out.

"Nothing. But did you know that antelope makes great sausage? Anything's better than grits. I didn't want you to forget Kansas with all the lavish Southern hospitality heaped on you last night. Or hasn't it bothered you?"

For a moment Barbara was silent. "Of course, it hasn't! I must admit that last night's ball made me homesick for the old days. But I belong with Charlie. Wherever he is, that's where I'm happiest."

"Well, I hope the fancy luncheon at this classy new hotel won't turn your head, Barbie. Who'd you say was inviting you?"

"Not only me, Bitsy. Us . . . you and me. And it was Mrs. Maxwell. She and my mother were old friends. It was a fine gesture on her part to ask us to come."

"Of course. Now just pull up a chair and eat. Then you'd best entertain the widow for the rest of the morning. She's pinin' for the sight of you, she says. When do you see Lawyer Cornwall?"

"Friday, I hope. I'll be glad when our business is settled and we can go back home." She hesitated slightly on the last word. What was "home" to her now? Here, where she'd been born and spent her childhood, or out on the lonely prairie as Charlie's wife? She shook her head fiercely and tackled the stack of buckwheat cakes.

As she went into the dining room, the rain still drummed on the eaves and pattered down the panes. The magnolia bushes on the west side of the house lifted their wet faces. She stood by the window and leaned against the sill. The widow came to stand beside her.

"Almost like old times, isn't it, Barbara?" she said softly. "A good day for white-washin' kitchens, it is. But now my family is gone and my house must go to ruin. Do you remember the day Matthew brought you into town to spend the day with me? It was rainin', but the two of you pulled on your oilskins and boots and splashed to the market for fresh ears of sweet corn. Y'all were a-laughin' and a-gigglin' like a pair of happy children. It did my heart good just to hear you. Sometimes I think Matthew will come in any moment, and everythin' will be the way it was . . . " Her words trailed off sadly.

Barbara slipped an arm round the thin, drooping shoulders. "Mrs. Potter, those days are gone. They can never come back. For whatever reason, the Lord took away those days and we must believe He knows best."

"But to take away my husband, and then my only son, your own betrothed!" the widow burst out bitterly jerking away. "What kind of God is He?"

"He says, 'But My ways are not your ways, nor your ways My ways.' He *has* promised He'll never forsake us. That's one of His sure promises."

"Then to take you away from me too, Barbara. If you'd just stay with me, it would be easier—"

"Stay with you Mrs. Potter? You know Charlie and I are married. There's no way—"

"Well, when y'all inherit the land from your father's brother, you and Charlie can come back here to live, and I'll see you sometimes. Promise me?"

With a sigh Barbara turned away from the dreary window. How could she explain to Matthew's mother that she and Charlie wanted to expand their land, to build a ranch? And that her place was with her husband, even if it was out on the vast prairies?

She knew the woman was lonely, but to cling to memories of Barbara and her dead son was not the way to solve her problems.

"I'd better get dressed for the luncheon with Mrs. Maxwell," she said after an awkward pause. "Bitsy and I will fix a lunch for you before we leave. What would you like?"

"Remember how the darkies fixed yam pies?" she asked. "It's been so long since I had one. There's a recipe book in the cupboard drawer if you need it."

As she scurried into the kitchen a sudden wave of nausea hit her again. *What's wrong with me? I can't get sick now!* she thought. Then just as quickly, it left again.

She and Bitsy worked on yam pies according to the recipe book they found in the drawer. In less that two hours the pies were cooling on the kitchen table for Mrs. Potter's lunch while the girls were dressing for their luncheon.

At 11:30, Barbara and Bitsy, wearing their brightest cotton prints, waited for the Maxwell carriage. The rain had slowed to an intermittent wetting shower as they were assisted into the shabby, black vehicle.

The ride to the Calhoun House was short. The hotel certainly eclipsed the Kimball House, which had burned. A corps of efficient clerks and servants swarmed through the crowded lobby, and a waiter immediately ushered them into an elaborate dining room in the basement. It was the last word in architecture and equipment. Swinging above each table was an improvised fly brush manipulated by a small, black boy. In the center of each table stood a revolving disc-like arrangement, its surface broad enough to hold salt and pepper, butter, cheeses and preserves.

Mrs. Maxwell waited for them at the far end of the room and rose when Barbara and Bitsy walked between the tables toward her. She greeted them cheerfully and told them to be seated.

"It's good to see you back in Atlanta," Mrs. Maxwell said graciously. "I'm so glad you have returned. I trust you're enjoyin' your stay with Widow Potter?"

"She has been most kind to take us in," Barbara said. "Of course, I'm here on business. As soon as it's finished, we . . . we plan to go back to Kansas."

"It's too bad fate took such a cruel turn and snatched away your betrothed," Mrs. Maxwell said with deep sympathy.

"But we cannot question God's ways," Barbara began quietly. "I—"

"It all worked out for the best," Bitsy cut in, trying to stifle a giggle with her napkin. "If Cousin Barbie hadn't come to Kansas, she'd never have met Charlie, you see. Charlie, the 'Knight of the Cottonwood'."

"Indeed!" Mrs. Maxwell exclaimed incredulously. "And what

157

sort of . . . royalty is that?"

Barbara glanced sharply at Bitsy, whose blue eyes danced with mischief. "He rode up on a white steed one day and snatched Barbie away from White Turkey, the Indian brave, as dashing and gallant as any Rebel cavalry."

Mrs. Maxwell jerked her head as if in consternation. "But, of course," she said stiffly. Then she paused. "Shall we order? The beef roasts are excellent and the vegetable side dishes most delectable."

The next few moments passed with small talk. Mrs. Maxwell, in trying to extol the virtues of the "new" Atlanta, soared away in describing the theater with its brilliant, sparkling comedies, farces, singing and dancing, and dramas such as *The Miser* and *Loan of a Lover*. She pointed out a small, gray, moustached man at the next table.

"That's Dr. Eli Griffin, the doctor at the city's smallpox hospital. There's been a rash of smallpox here, but Atlanta's Medical College is graduatin' its first class of young doctors this month. And last spring, the sport of baseball came to Atlanta," she gushed. "To Captain Tom Burnett, proprietor of the Ice House on Wall Street, goes the credit for introducin' this great American sport through the Atlanta Baseball Club. Although the players were as green as grass when they started, hundreds of spectators come out to see them swing the willow stick. They've even been playin' other teams. You should see their natty uniforms of white caps, white flannel shirts and black trousers. People have been amazed at these wonderful players, and there's even a brass band that plays at the games."

She paused dramatically, as if to rest on Atlanta's laurels in emerging victoriously from the throes of war.

Bitsy drew in a quick, short breath. "How about that! Baseball in shell-shocked Atlanta already. But of course, baseball's been around for a long time. Ever since the Bible days."

Barbara opened her mouth to protest, then closed it quickly, knowing Bitsy was in a whimsical mood.

"Oh? Surely it isn't *that* old, Miss Moore!" Mrs. Maxwell

paused to tuck a white linen napkin around her lap.

"I'm sure you've read the Bible account of Isaac and Rebekah, and how his servant found her walking to the well with a *pitcher*?"

"What Bitsy means," Barbara cut in quickly, knowing Mrs. Maxwell would take her cousin for a crude, country bumpkin, "what she means is—"

"What I mean is . . . life goes on, no matter where one lives . . . even in Kansas," Bitsy retorted sweetly.

"Well, really!" the older woman half-muttered under her breath.

The waiter brought their lunch of thickly sliced roast beef and succulent new potatoes smothered in creamed asparagus.

Barbara's stomach rebelled at the asparagus and she took a sip of water quickly. *Was it the water that had made her feel queasy since she had arrived?* she wondered.

She finished eating her lunch before Bitsy and Mrs. Maxwell did. As they chattered away between bites, she began to think about Friday, when she was to see Mr. Cornwall. She hoped that Uncle Alex's property settlement would be accomplished quickly.

When the luncheon was over, Barbara thanked Mrs. Maxwell, who turned to her and took her hands.

"I trust after your property settlement you'll come to live in our fair city with your . . . with Charlie, of course. It will be good to see more of you. You remind me so much of Candace, your dear mother."

"Barbie belongs to our prairies now, Mrs. Maxwell," Bitsy said with a smirk. "Or didn't you know?"

"Bitsy!" Barbara said sharply. "After all, I did grow up here and . . . and I have a few ties left. But of course, that will depend upon how Uncle Alex's will reads."

When the girls were on their way home, Bitsy turned to Barbara. "What did you mean? Do you have famous last thoughts about leaving this country behind, Barbara? I thought you wanted to help Charlie Warren build his ranch."

"I . . . I do. It's just . . . well, I'm having a good time here.

You were right, Bitsy! It's fun meeting people again. You've no idea how lonely our little soddy is. When I compare the two, sometimes I'm so torn." Barbara couldn't go on. What *did* she feel toward Atlanta? It was hard to shake off her feelings of belonging here where she had grown up.

But of course, the idea was ridiculous. She knew she'd go back to Kansas, back to Charlie and Willie to live on the flat, vast plains in the little soddy that stood bleak and alone. She shook off her feelings of doubt.

On Friday afternoon Barbara dressed herself carefully. She coiled her rich brown hair into its bun. Shaking out the shabby green-sprigged delaine, she decided to heat the flat irons and press the wrinkles from the full skirt, for she must make a good impression on the lawyer.

Bitsy picked up a pair of long, gold earrings. "Here. Wear these. They'll give you class. We don't want Mr. Cornwall to think you ain't fitten to inherit all that luscious land. No doubt, Mrs. Maxwell already thinks I'm rude and crude and uncouth. And what a sassy companion and example I am to you!"

Barbara grinned as Bitsy fastened them to her earlobes. "Well, you were rather saucy to her the other day. I only want what rightfully belongs to me. If . . . there's a question," she paused, a slight frown between her eyes. "But the lawyer wouldn't have sent for me if there was. Would he?"

Just then the carriage pulled up and Barbara hurried to the door. It wasn't Toby after all, and Barbara was disappointed. But Toby was free now. And it was best to cut the ties to her old life.

The team of grays trotted down the street to the National Hotel, Atlanta's leading hostelry. It was even more elaborate than the Calhoun, if that was possible. Within minutes Barbara was ushered into Lawyer Cornwall's suite of offices on the second floor. The fine mahogany desk shone with polish.

The lawyer was short of stature, with a bristling beard and a pugnacious look in his gray eyes. He rose from behind his desk as Barbara came into the room, and pulled out a chair for her.

"Here, Mrs. Warren. Please be seated."

After they had exchanged a few pleasantries, he returned to his desk and opened a thick, manila envelope.

"I suppose we might as well proceed with our business. Please tell me about your father and what you remember of your Uncle Alex."

Barbara told him of her father's plantation, and his untimely death at the beginning of the war when he had taken over a troop of Rebel soldiers, how the field darkies had fled, and how the fine antebellum house and barns mysteriously went up in flames.

"Mother and I moved to Atlanta then, where she learned that my father had mortgaged the plantation heavily to help finance the Rebel cause. My brother, Whatley, had died, and we tried to eke out a living by whatever means we could. We had saved several heirlooms which we sold for food and clothes. Mother, suffering from shock and discouragement, died not long afterwards.

"Uncle Alex and I had never been very close. He knew he would soon be called upon to serve in some capacity in the war, so he wrote to Mother's brother, Daniel Moore, in Kansas. Uncle Daniel and Aunt Prudy promptly invited me to come live with them. After Matthew Potter died, I thought my life was over. Then I fell in love with Charlie Warren."

He nodded and began to shuffle the papers on his desk. Then he cleared his throat. "It all agrees with what Alex Temple had in his journal. Now, the terms of his will state what he had in mind. As you know, he left no direct heirs. But he left the will. It took me a long time to find you."

Barbara waited for him to continue. He shuffled through his neat stack of papers again, as if stalling for some time. Then he cleared his throat once more.

"According to this will . . . I'll read it aloud to you in a minute . . . he wanted you to have his property, a substantial piece, though not an elaborate one, which lies about two miles south of Atlanta. It's quite run down but not beyond repair. There are 800 acres of land. However, there's a stipulation."

Drawing a tense breath, Barbara moistened her dry lips. *I wish he'd get on with it, so I can dispose of the place and leave,* she thought.

"What . . . what is this stipulation?" she ventured finally.

"That you are to live there and farm it as he had. If you don't, you must sign away all rights to it. It then goes to a distant cousin, Elmer Dossett."

"S-sign away rights to it?" she whispered raggedly. "You mean, I must occupy his place, if I accept the terms of his will?"

"That is correct. Here. Let me read it to you."

Barbara sat stunned as the lawyer waded through all the legal jargon and jumble of "whereases." She felt the blood drain from her face. Did this mean that to inherit Uncle Alex's property, she and Charlie must move here? But that was preposterous! She knew it would create a real upheaval in their lives to leave Kansas and come back to what had been "home" to her for 16 years. The idea boggled her mind. Perhaps she could do it. But what of Charlie and Willie? She must consider them.

"Well? Is there a problem with these terms, Mrs. Warren?" His bristled beard wiggled.

Slowly Barbara rose from her chair. She didn't realize how weak she was until her knees shook and she had to steady herself against the desk.

"Let me . . . think about it. I cannot give you an answer right now."

"All right." Cornwall nodded. "I'll give you three days to decide. But no longer. My carriage will take you out to the place, if you care to see it first."

Barbara gave a weak nod as she staggered to the door and opened it with unsteady hands. Then she walked outside into the bright, August sunlight.

CHAPTER 22

Stepping into Mr. Cornwall's carriage, Barbara leaned over to the driver and tapped his shoulder.

"I'd like to drive out to Alex Temple's plantation, please."

The man nodded briefly, clucked to the team, and soon they clattered down the street. Her eyes blurred with tears as the impact of the will's stipulation surged through her. She was to move onto the place if she were to inherit it. How could she possibly do that? She belonged to Charlie, and his dream was to build a ranch on the fertile, grassy plains. How could she ask him to leave his dream and come to live in what was an alien land to him? It was unthinkable. And yet . . .

They had left the outskirts of Atlanta now, and the carriage wheels rumbled southward. Barbara peered at the scenery. The sky was still and blue, and high cauliflower clouds seemed to hang overhead without movement. It was a windless, wide landscape with low foothills beyond the misty green of pasture. Certainly it looked tame compared to the wild, windy prairies of Kansas.

Plantations that once stood proud and fine in magnificent groves of enormous trees had grayed and blurred into piles of blackened rubble. It seemed so cruel, yet mercifully, not all plantations had suffered complete ruin. She realized that farmers who could no longer make a living without slaves to till the cotton had moved to Atlanta, and some farmland lay idle.

Before long, the carriage slowed and the driver turned into a long, familiar drive. The huddle of buildings, still intact, looked weathered and abandoned, the cottonfields bare and overgrown with weeds. Lush pastures, green from recent rains, stretched away beyond the gray barns. The house, although rather plain and drab after years of neglect, seemed spacious and commodious compared to the tiny two-roomed soddy on the plains.

"With Charlie and Willie's help," she murmured to herself, "the place could flourish into the kind of farm we'd be proud of."

Yet she doubted that neither Charlie nor Willie would be happy here. Still, perhaps if Charlie considered its possibilities.

With a sigh, Barbara shook her head. She didn't know what to do.

"Let's go back to town," she told the driver who grunted in response as he turned the carriage around and they headed between the broken picket fences down the lane.

Just then she spied Tullie Smith's plantation along the tree-lined, wooded trail, and her heart quickened. Several times in the past she had visited the plain style home, typical of the early-to-middle 19th century farm.

"Oh, let's stop for a few minutes," Barbara said to the driver. "I want to visit Miss Tullie while I'm here."

As the carriage drew up before the house, memories stirred in Barbara of visits she'd paid to the sprightly Miss Tullie. The house, as she remembered it, was characterized by two front rooms downstairs and two above, with a shed extending from the rear to form two more downstairs rooms. She recalled the "parson's room," added later where visitors or traveling ministers were frequent guests.

After the driver had tied up the team at the hitching post, Barbara hopped down and hurried up the bricked path to the wooden steps and onto the wide front porch, where an old wooden rocker swayed gently in the mild August breeze.

She rapped sharply on the solid oak door and heard a quiet rustle as a tiny aproned woman opened it. Miss Tullie, her eyes wide and green under the fringe of gray hair, stared at her for a moment. Then a smile lit the merry face.

"If it isn't Miss Barb'ra Temple. Why, bless my soul, but it's good to see you. Do come in!"

As Barbara stepped over the threshold, the rich aroma of aged, polished wood rushed to greet her. The bare, wooden floor creaked beneath her feet as Miss Tullie hugged her soundly. The furnishings were as plain and simple as she remembered them. Two fireplaces on either side provided heat in winter.

"My, what a treat to see you, Miss Barb'ra!" Miss Tullie gushed. "You must come into the kitchen for a cup of tea."

With a pang, Barbara thought of Aunt Prudy as the tiny figure scudded ahead toward the large, roomy kitchen. Like most plantation homes, the kitchen was separate from the main part of the house to keep the heat from the other rooms during the summer season.

The aroma of herbs that hung from the ceiling rafters was as she remembered it. Homemade barrels stored with food items such as corn, sugar and flour lined the pantry. Beyond the house were the large, log barn and smokehouse.

Bustling to the huge, black cookstove, Miss Tullie shoved a tea kettle to the front burner and stirred the ashes into a bright blaze. She chattered about trying to keep the plantation but having to sell most of the land to live. Still, it was lonely all by herself, she admitted.

"I baked some tea cakes this very mornin' just hopin' someone would drop by," she said, shaking the grate to hurry up the blaze. "Pull up a chair and tell me what brings you back to Gawgia. I was given to understand you had left Atlanta to live elsewhere after your uncle went into the army."

"Yes, Miss Tullie, just before Uncle Alex was called up to duty, I went to Kansas to live with my mother's brother Daniel Moore and Aunt Prudy and their family. I've been married to

Charlie Warren for a year. Now I came back because Barrister Cornwall informed me that Uncle Alex has willed his land to me. I've just been down to see . . ." She paused as she pulled up the chair and sat down gratefully. The ride had tired her more than she had realized.

"Why, bless my heart, that's marvelous! Of course, it's been real run down and needs a heap of fixin' up. The land's laid idle for the past few years, too. It'll be fine to have you come back here. I sure could use a neighbor."

"Uh," Barbara paused to clear her throat. "You see, I . . . my husband, Charlie, and I had hoped to sell the plantation and use the money for a ranch in Kansas. But it seems the will reads I'm to live here if I want to inherit it. If not, some distant cousin will be the heir."

"So what's the problem? Surely you and your Charlie will take over, won't you?"

Barbara took a deep breath. "I . . . don't know. You see, Charlie's a midwesterner. He came to Kansas from Illinois. I don't know if he'll want to move out here and learn an entire new way of farming."

"Fiddlesticks!" Miss Tullie set out a pair of dainty Staffordshire china cups and filled them with bubbling water. The heady fragrance of mint and thyme wafted from the steaming teapot.

"You belong to the South, Miss Barb'ra. You were created to keep the old Southern charm aflame! Your mother would've wanted you to come back here and live where you was brought up, wouldn't she? Alex Temple's plantation house needs a woman like you to bring it back to life. I'll be downright blessed to have you for a neighbor again, Miss Barb'ra Temple."

"But I can't be sure—"

"Nonsense! You tell that young man of yours this is where you was meant to live, not some raw heathen country crawlin' with Indians and buffalo!"

Barbara sipped her tea slowly, grateful for its soothing flavor. The tea cakes were tasty and crunchy with sesame seeds and ground persimmons. How charming and complete this kitchen was compared to the tiny sodhouse with its topsy stove. She knew she'd have a staunch friend and good neighbor in Miss Tullie, although she'd never forget the implacable Mame Probst. But here were people who had survived a country battered by war and deprivation. She allowed herself to imagine how, in time, the plantation would respond to Charlie's and Willie's capable hands, more land than they'd ever dreamed of owning in Kansas. And it was hers—if she wanted it.

She couldn't see herself returning to Kansas when they could make a fresh start in a land now booming with new energy, new life.

Sighing deeply, she set down her teacup. "Well, Miss Tullie, I can't promise this will happen, but if I can persuade my husband to come to Georgia, we might become neighbors again." Slowly she got to her feet. "It's time I drive back to Atlanta. The driver will be waiting."

Miss Tullie hugged her warmly and beamed. "I shall certainly look forward to seein' you back here before long. I just know y'all be back!"

She followed Barbara to the door and down the brick path to the waiting carriage. The driver was asleep, and when Barbara called out to him, he awoke with a jerk.

"Yes'm," he muttered. "It's time to move on."

It's time to move on. The words haunted Barbara on the way back to town. Perhaps he was right. She had struggled about her decision, but with a new determination, she knew she must write to Charlie right away. Soon they would come to Georgia and begin a new life.

Bitsy and Widow Potter weren't in when Barbara reached the little cottage. They had probably gone to the market for more food. Without a word she went to the bedroom, drew out her writing pad, and began a letter to Charlie. It was best for them all, she wrote, a large place to farm, cultural opportunities for Willie. And loneliness would no longer dog her.

"Lord, surely this is Your will," she whispered as she sealed the letter. "You have surely provided this new beginning for us." As she walked to the door, another wave of nausea swept over her, and she held onto the door jamb before letting herself out.

Her legs shook as she pushed herself down the few blocks to the mail pickup box. She dropped the letter into the slot and dragged herself back to the house, so exhausted that every step was an effort.

She was about to lie down on the shabby sofa when she heard the slam of the kitchen door and Bitsy's lilting laughter and lively chatter.

"I'll bet you peanuts to sunflowers the potatoes we grow in our Kansas soil are twice as big as these spuds. Look how scrawny these are!"

"Maybe so. But our peanuts are a good crop even in these hard times. Have you ever eaten any roasted peanuts?"

"Can't say that I have. By the way, I wonder if Barbie's back yet?" she chattered on. "She's been out a good long spell. She hasn't looked too pert these past few days, you know. And I'm a bit worried about her."

Barbara passed a hand over her face. *Pert* wasn't the word for the way she was feeling. *Miserable* would be a better word.

"Barbie?" Bitsy called out. "You back?"

"Yes, I'm here. I . . . I asked the driver to take me out to the plantation. I . . . somehow wanted to see it." Barbara's voice sounded weak to her own ears. Her mind fretted and scratched through her turmoil.

Mrs. Potter followed Bitsy into the front room. With a great effort, Barbara sat up.

"I . . . I wrote to Charlie and told him . . . we . . . we'll move here, as it's the only way I can inherit Uncle Alex's property."

Bitsy stopped abruptly and stared hard at her. "Barbie! You can't mean that!"

"It's the only way the land is available to me," she said in a tired voice.

"I think that's splendid!" Widow Potter cried, clapping her hands. "Now you'll visit me often, whenever you come to town!"

Bitsy flung off her bonnet and shook her butter-yellow head. "I don't believe it! Are you crazy? You know as well as I that Charlie will never agree to this."

"Why . . . not?" Barbara said slowly. Her head was reeling now. "Just think how sensible . . . it is. Here are 800 acres of good farmland, and a house that's three times the size of that . . . that confounded two-roomed soddy! And here are *people*. I've already written—"

"You didn't!" Bitsy shrieked. "You mean, you actually told him to leave Kansas and move out here? Barbara Warren, are you daft?"

"I . . . I thought it over and—"

"Did you remember to pray about it, Cousin? Make sure this is what God wants?"

Barbara tried to steady herself, but the room was spinning all around her now, and she felt herself moving into a black chasm. It whirled faster and faster.

"God?" Where was He? She groped with her fingers as if to grab His arms.

I can't think any more, she thought. "It . . . it's best for us." She didn't know if she was speaking aloud, but suddenly her consciousness had become a speck of agony in a whirl of hot darkness. And then everything went black.

CHAPTER 23

Like the wail of a distant locomotive, Barbara Warren sensed faraway sounds that penetrated her subconscious. She clutched at consciousness but it seemed to fade away with each feeble spark of awareness.

Then she heard distinct voices: "It isn't . . . smallpox is it?" "She's been tired . . . tired . . . tired . . ." Words echoed through her weary brain. Smallpox . . . the word seeped into her befuddled mind.

With great effort she opened her eyes. Everything was a blur before her. As she batted her eyelids, Bitsy's anxious face struggled to materialize, and Widow Potter's startled expression swam beside it. Then she was aware of an elderly, kind-faced man bending over her, his hand on her wrist.

"She's coming around!" a voice whispered somewhere in the background. Barbara blinked and tried to raise her head, but gentle hands pushed her back onto the sofa pillow.

"I . . . what's . . . what am I doing here?" she muttered raggedly. "Who . . . are you?"

The man stroked her hand softly. "I'm Dr. Griffin. You passed out and your family is worried about you."

"What's the matter . . . with me? S-s-smallpox?"

"I don't think so. I've taken care of a good many people in the smallpox hospital here. You don't have the symptoms. But if you don't mind, I'll make a more thorough examination."

At least it isn't smallpox, Barbara told herself, feeling quite conscious and aware now. After the doctor tested and probed and asked several questions, he leaned back with a benign smile.

"Well, young lady, you've been under a tremendous strain. But that's not all. It seems you're going to have a child, possibly around March or April."

"A . . . baby?" Barbara gasped as she tried to sit up on the sofa. "But—" she scowled. Babies die on the prairies. Cousin Rosie's Sammie, Eva Mae's newborn, Nellie McNeer. *I don't know if I want a child.*

"You're not pleased?" Dr. Griffin inquired in a solemn voice. "Most young women would be ecstatic for their first."

Barbara shook her head, stunned. The idea was so preposterous. Mrs. Potter beamed down at her.

"Barb'ra, it will be almos' like havin' a grandchild! I myself will take care of you every minute. Y'all can count on that. Why, it'll open up a whole new world for me!"

Bitsy stood silent to one side, her face taut. Barbara knew her cousin was deeply disappointed in her for some reason.

"I'd hoped for a family of boys, and maybe a girl or two to help you" were Charlie's words that came to her mind from the conversation they had after the McNeer girl and the Parker baby were buried in their little God's Acre. No! She shook the memory away and brushed a hand over her eyes. It was hard to believe. A baby. She didn't want a baby. Not on the prairie. Then she remembered her decision to stay in Atlanta.

" . . . and you'll feel better in a few weeks," Dr. Griffin was saying as he rose to his feet. "I want you to exercise and live a normal life. Your young man is very lucky to have such a fine-looking wife as a mother for his young'uns. If you need me again, just call." He reached for a shabby felt hat, his black satchel and started for the door. Mrs. Potter followed him out.

As Barbara swung her feet down from the sofa to the floor she looked around. The giddiness was fading. The room looked the same, yet everything had changed. It wasn't at all the way it had been before she received all the news of this day. Bitsy stood silent and thoughtful by the window. *I know I've let her down,* Barbara thought. *But—*

"Bitsy," she called. "I . . . I'm sorry I've failed you. To tell you the truth . . . I almost wondered if I hadn't made a mistake in writing Charlie. But this . . . this child makes a difference," her voice trailed away.

Her cousin whirled away from the window. "Well, it should!" she flared. "I'm sure Charlie's wanted a family. You survived a hard year in Western Kansas. The hearty air of the prairie breeds strength. So what are you scared of?"

Was it true? Was she afraid? Did the strength and vigor of the raw country instill character and depth? She didn't know. It had never occured to her that she was going to have a baby. Suddenly she knew she wanted it with all her heart. Now she was glad she'd decided to stay in Atlanta. Here were doctors to help the baby get a good start. Wasn't that worth considering?

All during the evening meal Mrs. Potter bubbled with plans for the newcomer, with Bitsy countering her every idea.

"Whose baby is this, Mrs. Potter? Yours? Or Barbie's?" she retorted with fervor.

Barbara retired early. The day's events had worn her out, and her body cried for rest. When she lay down she fell asleep instantly and slept soundly through the night.

In the morning she felt refreshed. A new vigor was in her step as she came into the kitchen for breakfast.

"Now don't y'all lift a finger for anything," Mrs. Potter clucked helping her to a chair. "Be careful."

Barbara shrugged off the grip. "I feel better today, Mrs. Potter. The doctor said to live a normal life. After I've had a hearty breakfast, I'm going for a walk."

"Bravo!" Bitsy said from the stove. "When you came to Kansas you were the prissy Southern belle, but you've done a good job of turning into a frontier woman. And don't you forget it!"

Barbara didn't answer. Bitsy didn't understand. She didn't know if she did either.

Half an hour later, she stepped outside. The heavy, warm somnolence seemed invigorating as she strolled down the street. Tall, stiff hollyhocks reared maroon and cream-colored heads against the picket fence. Aromas of proud sheaths of gladioli mingled with the blend of drying grass, like the tangy scent of coming autumn.

I should enjoy this lovely scenery, she thought, *but today I'm not sure of my feelings.* Charlie's face loomed before her, his eyes accusing. Was Bitsy right? Of course, the baby would have every advantage here.

The little white-steepled Presbyterian church just down the street beckoned her, and she quickened her footsteps. Perhaps if she slipped in to pray, she'd find the answer to her perplexing problems. Her baby should have every advantage, she reminded herself again. Yet what Charlie wanted mattered, too.

Walking quietly up the steps, she stepped inside and down the carpeted aisle toward the front. The scent of furniture polish seemed to augment the holy hush that fell over the dark pews and the rubbed chancel rail.

Kneeling down, Barbara held her head in her hands. "Oh, precious Lord, what shall I do?" she prayed. "Have I made a mistake in telling Charlie to move here? But I have to consider more than myself . . . there's Charlie's baby now. Our baby needs the best possible care. Yet, what of my husband? Bitsy seems to think he wouldn't consider moving. I . . . I think she may be right."

She began to cry great tears that cut shiny paths down her cheeks. "Dear Lord, what shall I do?" she cried again. She felt so torn, so troubled.

As she heard the rustle of a presence beside her, she raised her head. The pastor stood there, looking at her kindly.

"I'm Robert Mallard. Can I help in any way?" he asked quietly.

Slowly she rose to her feet and then dropped into the nearest pew. He came and sat beside her.

"Are you troubled, Miss?" he asked again.

Barbara gave a quick nod as she swallowed her tears. "I . . . I don't quite know what to do. I'm Barbara Warren of Kansas, and I came to Georgia when I learned that my uncle had left his plantation to me. I'd planned to sell it so I could help my husband, Charlie, buy the ranch in Kansas that he's dreamed of. But—"

"But what?"

"The will states that if I'm to inherit, I must settle on the place. I . . . I love Charlie very much. And I know it would be hard to persuade him to leave his dreams behind and come here. Now I've just learned that we're going to have . . . a child. Charlie had counted on . . . on a son . . . a family of sons to help build the ranch. But when I think of all the advantages here—good medical care, schooling, culture—I . . . I just don't know what . . . what God's will is in all of this!"

"Do you know Christ as your Savior?" he asked gently.

"Oh, yes! I accepted His salvation several years ago and it has been our aim, Charlie's and mine, to follow Him, to bear fruit. Without God I couldn't have made it! But the way seems so confusing now, and I don't know which way to turn."

"Then turn to Him with your cares. He promises rest to the weary, peace to the troubled soul. Do you want to come back here to live? For yourself? For the baby? What of your wedding vows you made to your husband?"

Barbara leaned forward and cradled her aching head in her arms. "Yes, I recall the ceremony," she said haltingly. "There was this Quaker elder in the log church who asked if . . . if I'd be faithful 'on the Trail and on the Plain' . . . and I knew it was forever with Charlie, wherever God led. But now . . ."

Pastor Mallard began to page through his Bible. Then he said, "In Luke 9 it says, 'No man, having put his hand to the plow and looking back, is fit for the kingdom of God.' Barbara, do you honestly want to look back, come back here, if your husband would be unhappy? Wouldn't the Lord see to it that your child would have what it needs on the Plains? If that is where your husband wants to live?"

For a long time Barbara studied her trembling hands. Was she "looking back," wanting the life here where she'd grown up, where her old friends and ties were? Was she thinking of the baby now? Or was this an excuse? Hadn't she promised Charlie to go wherever he went, in spite of Indians, hot prairies, blizzards and loneliness?

Sobbing, she covered her face with her hands. "Oh, I've been selfish! I thought I was doing this for Charlie, for our baby, but I was really doing it for myself. I was afraid to trust God for what lies ahead. Dear God, forgive me!" She wept with strangled sobs of anguish.

Then she drew a dainty, worn handkerchief from her handbag, blew her nose and rose to her feet. She stretched out her hand and said, "Thank you, Pastor Mallard. I know the answer now."

"God bless you, Sister. And God bless Charlie and the child, too," he added reverently.

I must hurry back to Kansas to tell Charlie, she decided as she left the church and marched down the street. She felt an urgency she hadn't known before. There was no time to lose.

"Bitsy!" she called out as she closed the front door behind her. "Let's pack up today and leave first thing in the morning. We're going back to Kansas after I stop at Mr. Cornwall's and give up my inheritance."

Bitsy hurried toward her and threw out her arms. "Oh, Barbie, so you've come to your senses." She grinned wickedly. "Remember I told you that you loved Charlie Warren? You didn't even realize it! I guess you really need me to look after you."

Widow Potter bustled up beside her. "What's this nonsense you're sayin'? What of the baby?" she cried. "He belongs here. You must let him grow up where he'll have the best trainin', and a chance to be schooled properly. And what of me? Don't I count? After all, I am Matthew's mother!"

Barbara paused. She was feeling very tired again. Gently she laid her hands upon Mrs. Potter's shoulders. "Of course you do. But I'm married to Charlie. I doubt very much if he'd move here. Isn't the Lord able to provide the right care for our children wherever we live? I'm sorry, but I know now that my place is with my husband in Kansas."

The woman sagged and drew herself away. "I . . . I s'pose I should've realized you . . . y'all changed when you married your Charlie. That my dreams of havin' you back was too good to be true."

"It's like Barbie said. We'd better get back," Bitsy chirped, "before Charlie gets that letter!"

"Oh, yes. We must hurry!" Barbara echoed. "My only regret is that I can't bring Charlie the money I'd hoped. And I'm not able to pay you as much as I had hoped to," she said looking over at Mrs. Potter. "I'm giving the land to Elmer Dossett."

"Knowing Charlie, I don't think he'll care, as long as he has you," Bitsy said. "C'mon Barbie, let's start packing."

As Barbara started wearily for the bedroom, Widow Potter's eyes narrowed. "I wish you'd never come back here," she muttered bitterly.

Barbara looked her straight in the eyes, squared her shoulders and walked through the doorway of the bedroom. She began to take down the dresses from the hooks in the closet.

After a brief consultation with Bitsy, she returned to Mrs. Potter's side to give the widow an envelope containing a few dollars from the money Uncle Daniel had given them from his sale of buffalo bones.

"Here, Mrs. Potter. It's all the money we can give you in appreciation for your letting us stay here with you. I had hoped it would have been more than this," Barbara said gently as she handed her the envelope. "Thank you."

Without a word or a glance toward Barbara's face, Mrs. Potter took the envelope from her hand and walked back through the hallway.

CHAPTER 24

The next day passed in a blur. Although the packing didn't take long, Barbara was worn out before the job was done.

Bitsy sat on the bed and counted the change in her little coin purse. "If we skimp on food, we'll have enough to get us home. The tickets are paid for, but—"

"I never knew that having a baby could make one feel so ragged."

"Well, Dr. Griffin did say it wouldn't last long. And that you've been under a lot of stress. Now square your shoulders and help me think. We need someone to take us to the train station, and we must get food. What I wouldn't give right now for some buffalo jerky to take along. That stuff sticks to your ribs, and it keeps for weeks."

Barbara laid on the bed and stared at the cracked ceiling. "Have you ever tasted it?"

"Didn't I tell you? Last fall White Turkey visited Joshua. He's quite a decent sort, Barbie, since he became a believer. Well, the two went hunting for two days! When they got back, there were wild ducks galore. White Turkey wanted Josh to have them all, but we persuaded him to keep some. That's when he gave us the jerky. Well, actually it was pemmican."

Barbara shook her head. "Pemmican? I've never heard of it."

Bitsy laughed and said, "Are you ready for this? Josh says

177

you need jerky to make pemmican. You take some jerky and pound it with a stone until it's powdery, almost like flour. Then you tamp the powder into a large rawhide bag and pour melted fat over it. Josh says it's the best food to take when you must travel light. It sticks to your ribs and gives you strength. I tasted it. Not bad at all. Pemmican's what we need!"

A wave of nausea swept over Barbara at the thought. "No, thank you. I'll just take my chances and starve," she said with a delicate snort.

"Oh, well, you Southerners can have your grits and I'll have my jerky. Still . . ." she added scooping up the coins and dropping them back into her purse. "We'll have to figure out how to stay alive until we get home."

"I've worried about it too," Barbara said a trifle wearily. "I'm asking the Lord to provide, especially after reading Philippians 4:19 this morning. It says, 'And my God shall supply all your needs according to His riches in glory through Christ Jesus.' Do you suppose we could pray about this?"

"Good girl. Let's pray," Bitsy replied.

The girls knelt next to the bed, side by side and took turns thanking God for bringing them safely to Atlanta and asking Him to help them on their return journey. When they stood up, they heard the rustle of Mrs. Potter's dress as she walked by their room.

"Now we better make sure we don't leave a thing behind when we go. About the only thing I'd gladly leave here is another of the widow's tales of woe."

Barbara snapped her reticule after checking to make sure her combs and pins were safely stashed in the side pocket.

"Remember, she has been good to let us stay here and invade her life, Bitsy. When we leave, she'll feel alone and forsaken again. She is someone I must remember in my prayers."

Bitsy looked at her sharply, "Any regrets, Barbie?"

"No." Barbara shook her head. "No regrets. But I still feel sorry for her."

"Not as sorry as she feels for herself. Let's see if we can hire someone to take us to the station if we cut out our lunches."

"But first I must stop at Mr. Cornwall's office." Barbara started for the door. "I must also see if she has enough food for the next few days. Perhaps she can get a small pension from Matthew's death. It'll help."

Bitsy grabbed Barbara's shoulders. "I can't believe how you've changed. When you came from Atlanta, all you cared about then was Barbara Temple. Now you are a new person. Well, let's go. It's time to move on."

It's time to move on. Those words again. Barbara's heart gave a sudden lift. This time the move would lead her to Charlie and Willie.

Bitsy grabbed her sunbonnet and hurried out the door as Barbara made her way to the little parlor. The widow was seated in her rocker, her eyes downcast.

"I hate to see you go, Barbara," she said bitterly. "But I guess nothing will convince y'all to stay."

"No." Barbara knelt down and laid her head in the widow's lap. "Nothing. My husband's waiting for me in Kansas. And somehow, by God's grace, you'll make it without me."

"You think so? You've been talkin' about God's love ever since you came here, child. You know, we Potters never were church folk. How . . . how can I have the same kind of faith you have? It . . . it's changed you. I could tell the minute you came. Y'all have a source of strength."

"Not *a* source, but *the* Source, Mrs. Potter. Christ died for our sins. By accepting the fact that God loves us and gave His only Son to save us, we can have the blessed hope, that eternal life, that knowing God brings. He'll care for you too, if you ask Him."

Mrs. Potter sat silently for some time, then she stroked Barbara's hair gently. "I'm going to start reading my Bible. It belonged to Matthew and was sent to me after he . . . died."

"Matthew had a Bible?" Barbara got to her feet. "Do you s'pose he read it?"

"I don't know, but he prob'ly did. It looks very worn. There was so much danger."

At that moment Bitsy breezed through the door. "Get your

179

bonnet on, Barbie. Our chariot waiteth to take us to the train."

"How did you manage on such short notice?"

"Oh, I have my ways. Actually, I went boldly to Pastor Mallard and told him we were in a real fix. He offered to take us as soon as he got his team hitched. So let's hustle."

Rather unsteadily Barbara followed Bitsy to the bedroom and picked up her reticule. She felt wobbly, but she was going home. Her discomfort wouldn't last forever.

Saying goodbye to the widow wasn't easy. The gaunt little woman wept brokenly when Barbara threw her arms around her.

"I'll write you, Mrs. Potter. And be sure to go to Pastor Mallard's church. He'll answer your questions."

Bitsy hugged Mrs. Potter briefly and rushed out to the shabby, gray carriage. The tall, graying pastor helped Barbara into the front seat after Bitsy had scrambled into the back. Then he hoisted the luggage into the boot and they were off. The new National Hotel was so near the train stop that pausing for Barbara to sign away her property took little time. She needed only to cross the street to meet the train.

Lawyer Cornwall dipped his pen into the inkwell and handed it to her when she told him why she had come.

"If you're sure you want to do this—" he began, stroking his beard.

"I know it's the right answer," she said simply.

"Then," he paused and drew out an envelope from his drawer, "take this. I'm sure you'll need it."

As Barbara opened the flap she saw a wad of crisp Confederate bills and she drew in her breath sharply.

"What . . . what's it for?" she stammered.

"It seems your uncle left some travel money for you. I sent you the tickets earlier, but here's some extra left over. Use it to pay for food for you and your cousin. I couldn't let you go back without providing for your sustenance, although I wish you could have stayed."

"Oh, Mr. Cornwall, how did you know we needed it?"

He smiled faintly. "A lawyer, if he's any good, must be

shrewd. God grant that you'll return to your lucky young man safely."

Barbara's heart lifted. So the Lord had heard their prayer almost before they had asked!

"About Widow Potter. Do you think she could receive some sort of pension from Matthew's death? She's almost penniless," Barbara said suddenly as she got to her feet.

"Possibly. I'll see what I can do. But you'd better go or you'll miss the train."

As she hurried across the street, Bitsy waited on the hard bench near the tracks, her blue sunbonnet pushed back from her head. Barbara shoved a handful of bills into her hands.

"Run to that little shop for a loaf of bread and some fruit. Please hurry!"

Bitsy's blue eyes widened. "Where did you get this money?"

"Lawyer Cornwall said Uncle Alex had left something for my travel. After he bought the tickets, this was left over. The Lord provided for our food, but hurry. I think I hear a train coming down the tracks!"

Jumping up, Bitsy scuttled toward the shop. "I'll be right back. Don't leave without me!"

"I won't!" Barbara shouted. She leaned back and closed her eyes. *I'm so tired*, she thought. *When I get on that train, I'll sleep all the way home. Maybe I won't even eat.*

Ten minutes later the train clanged and whistled to a stop. Barbara looked toward the shop anxiously and started for the coach. She hoped Bitsy would hurry. Moments later her cousin burst breathlessly through the crowd waving a large paper sack.

"I've bread and cold meat, and some apples and pears," she huffed. "Now let's hop on the train before it leaves without us!"

The station master came for their luggage and headed for the baggage car. He pointed to the coaches.

"Better hurry. This is only a brief stop."

Hanging onto Bitsy's free arm, Barbara followed her cousin to the cars. The conductor was helping the passengers, muttering, "Tickets, please," as they brushed past him. The two young women slid into a smooth leather seat that looked none too clean. Obviously the cinders and soot had not been cleared away.

Sinking deeply into the seat, Barbara closed her eyes wearily. *Hurry, hurry* she thought impatiently. *I hope we hurry. I must get back to Charlie before my letter reaches him.*

"Are you gonna sleep all the way home, Barbie?" Bitsy chattered, tucking the sack of food under the seat. "It won't bother you if I'm lonely as a turtle, will it? You just lean back and dream of Charlie and Willie, and that baby you're going to have."

"Yes," Barbara muttered drowsily. "Daniel Charles Warren. How does that sound?"

"Daniel? After my papa? He'll be so pleased. But dream on, my cousin. Someone left a paperback dime novel behind. I can read while you dream."

"All aboard?" came ringing through the station.

The train began to grunt and chug, and with a few shrill toots it rumbled down the tracks.

I'm leaving Atlanta behind, Barbara thought, *and I don't care. Once I'd have sold my eyeteeth for a chance to stay. Why does the way seem so awfully long?*

The jolting, rocking coach soon relaxed her as the familiar scenes rushed past. The low drone of the engine became a part of her senses, and she wanted only to wipe away the past week and feel Charlie's arms around her.

When the train jerked to a stop at the small country depot, Barbara awoke with a start. The seat beside her was empty. Bitsy! Where was her cousin?

She blinked as cinders blew into her face. Then she saw the butter-yellow hair across the aisle. Her cousin was talking animatedly to a young man with fair, tousled hair and gray-blue eyes that were puckered at the corners. When he smiled, it seemed to light up his craggy face.

With a sigh, Barbara turned to the open window. The sky was deep, vaulted blue, with trees rushing past, hanging heavily as if exhausted by the heat. Great soap sud clouds began to build up thunderheads in the west. She was aware of a sudden movement beside her as Bitsy bounced back into the seat, her blue eyes shining.

"Guess what, Barbie?" she whispered with an excited giggle. "I just met the most gorgeous young man!"

Barbara frowned slightly. *Will I have to chaperone my usually sensible cousin the rest of the way?* she mused.

"Bitsy, please stay here. I don't like to be left alone—"

"It's *Elizabeth*, Barbie. Please be careful to call me Elizabeth Moore. I'm no longer a child. This man I was telling you about—"

"The gorgeous one? I hope you won't pick up every handsome stranger you meet simply because I don't feel like talking!" she snapped.

"The man's name is Merritt Wallace, and he's traveling to Manhattan, Kansas you know, to teach at Bluemont Central College. Isn't that exciting? He was smiling at me across the aisle—"

"With a come-hither look, no doubt. And you fell for that old trick?"

"Oh, Barbie, please don't be stuffy. Merritt, well, we talked and talked while you were in your land of dreams. He . . . he loves the Lord, Barbie, and he wants to see more of me back in Kansas. Isn't that great?"

Barbara paused and glanced surreptitiously at the young man. She had to admit he appeared honorable, and perhaps he was the special young man Bitsy had been waiting for.

"All right," she said slowly. "When I'm asleep, I'll let you visit all you wish. Right now I'd like a bite to eat."

"What would you like? Sorry, I didn't bring grits."

"What's wrong with grits?"

Bitsy rolled her eyes. "I only hope they don't serve grits in heaven!"

She grabbed their bag of food, tore open the loaf of bread and slapped a chunk of boiled ham between two wedges of bread.

Barbara munched absently, watching Bitsy from the corner of her eyes. Her cousin had always been bubbly and full of life, but never had seemed so vivacious, so alive.

The sun lowered in the west and pale, pink streaks touched the windows of the moving train. The conductor lit the oil lamps and shadows began to flicker in the corners and ledges of the coach as the train lurched and jogged along the tracks.

Barbara picked up the pillow Widow Potter had insisted she take and leaned back in her seat. Sighing, she wondered if the trip would ever end.

If only my letter won't reach Charlie before I do, she thought. *Lord, please.*

She was aware that Bitsy had stashed away their food and again was conversing quietly across the aisle with the blond, young man.

Barbara had to admit that having Merritt Wallace on the same coach must have been in God's plan, for the young man took over the responsibility of looking after their travel needs.

"Since I'm going almost as far as you," he had said with a boyish grin, "I'll see that we all arrive safely. Changing trains can sometimes be confusing." He was checking a map with Bitsy, who seemed all absorbed in what he was saying.

Barbara slept much of the way to Vincennes and awoke only for meals. On the way to St. Louis, Merritt Wallace pointed out many features of interest.

"St. Louis was known as the apex of the fur trade," Barbara heard him say. "When trappers brought in furs from the West, they were shipped to eastern factories, especially beaver for tall hats. I believe Jedediah Smith and others were pioneers in the fur-trapping business. This was a scant 30 years or so ago. I hear that the city has made great strides in becoming a metropolis through the years, with many paved streets, churches and schools, as well as foundries and lumber businesses. Both roads and ferry boats are thriving." He paused as the train slowed with a few coughing spurts and a hiss of steam. "Well, here we are. Now we'll soon board the new railroad and be on our way to Kansas."

Barbara vaguely remembered that the new Missouri Pacific Railroad had been completed to Kansas. Although the train jostled and jogged, travel was less hectic than the slow, unpredictable travel by steamboat. In a few hours they would reach Kansas.

Cloud shadows moved over the fields, and a wan light fell weakly across the plains. She could see the shimmer of the wide Missouri River with green, tilled fields beyond. Here and there, columns of wood smoke feathered up from some chimney in a cabin hidden among the trees, and a sweetness drifted through the open coach windows. Bitsy leaned toward Barbara.

"You awake? I've notified Papa to meet us at Cottonwood Crossing. Of course, Merritt helped me."

"When was this? I didn't realize—"

"When we changed trains in St. Louis. You were so deliciously lazy sitting on the bench that I didn't want to disturb you. If having a baby makes you fuzzy, I pity poor Charlie. He might wish you'd stayed in Atlanta!"

"Whether he likes it or not, Bits . . . Elizabeth, I'm coming home. But I . . . I've felt so tired, so relieved, perhaps, that all I want to do is sleep. Just don't forget to wake me up when we reach Kansas."

"It would serve you right if I put you on the Butterfield Despatch and let you sleep all the way to Ellsworth. But never mind. I won't be as cruel as that. It's a good thing I decided to go with you, although how I survived Widow Potter's constant whining and nagging, I'll never know. And you must admit you needed my sage advice and loving care."

Barbara let out a soft sigh. "I do appreciate your having gone with me, and your father deserves a big hand for sending you. Although I know I've slept most of the way back, you've made yourself pretty scarce since you've met that devastating Professor Wallace!"

Bitsy chuckled. "I knew he'd charm you once you realized how indispensable he is. And, do you know, Barbie? He's promised to come up for Thanksgiving. I'm glad we've added on to the cabin." She paused and looked around. "I think we're coming toward Kansas City now. I must find Merritt before we stop."

The yellow Missouri River boiled endlessly along the foot of the bluff, its flood-washed sands spilling into the water. The sun was now below the horizon and the red glow at the rim of the world faded into pink. The train had stopped for wood and water at Jefferson City and Sedalia, and made a few brief stops at Warrensburg and Lee's Summit. Now it shrilled and began to slow between the dark arches of the hills that flanked the river near the Kansas border.

Barbara's heart bounded with excitement. Soon she'd be back on the prairies with Charlie and Willie. Perhaps only a few more nights. *I must pull myself together,* she mused. *I hope I'll stop being so everlastingly bone-tired.*

Before long the train jerked to a stop. Passengers were on their feet, jostling with hand luggage and shoving down the narrow aisle now dim in the yellow lantern light.

Bitsy took Barbara's arm and helped her toward the wide, open doorway where Merritt waited. He helped Barbara gently to the ground as she swayed dizzily, groping for his arm.

"Steady, Barbara," he cautioned. "Just hang on to me. We'll find our carriage and that will take me to the Butterfield stage stop."

Bitsy bid goodbye to Merritt at the stop as he waited for the Butterfield stage that led to Manhattan and Bluemont Colleges. Her cousin wept softly for miles afterwards, and Barbara soon ran out of words of consolation to help her. She placed a consoling arm around Bitsy and let her cry.

The Santa Fe stage seemed the same as the one on which she had come to Kansas three years before, except it had seemed like an alien vehicle then. The Santa Fe Trail angled southwestward. At times the stage screeched and swayed as the teams sprang over the road, stopping briefly at Gardner, the junction of the Santa Fe and Oregon Trails. Then on, on, on it rattled toward Baldwin and Burlingame.

Barbara watched the miles skim by, the endless acres of

white-starred prairies and buffalo grass billowing in the ever-present wind.

"Well, Kansas hasn't lost its eternal breezes since we left," Barbara murmured as conversation dwindled. Thoughts of what lay ahead of them seemed to occupy their minds.

Bitsy blew her nose. "You didn't expect it to, did you? Anyway, it doesn't seem so awfully far from Manhattan. Looks like we're coming into Council Grove now."

"I suppose it's still as it was when we came through here a few weeks ago. I wonder if your father will be here to meet the stage?"

"Didn't I tell you? Merritt wired ahead to say we'd be going on to Cottonwood Crossing. It's not so far for him to pick us up. I hope he got the message."

"Your young man is quite resourceful."

"That's what I've been trying to tell you. Well, soon we'll be home," Bitsy said. "Put on your best Sunday grin in case the family's there to meet the stage."

Why was it taking so long? Barbara worried. Now that they were nearly home, time seemed to run on forever. She closed her eyes and willed them to sleep.

When she awoke the sun had lowered toward the west. Soft rose, tender green and misty lavender filled the lengthening shadows of the twilight prairie, and the world, for a moment, was rose-hued like the sunset's afterglow. As the stage slowed, Barbara saw they were coming into Cottonwood Crossing. The huddle of buildings looked warm and inviting.

When it jerked to a stop, Barbara blinked wide awake. Gathering up her skirts and her reticule, she took the driver's arm as she stepped to the ground. Bitsy hopped off after her. Uncle Daniel was waiting on his wagon.

Then Barbara's heart stopped. There stood Charlie, his dark curls tumbling over his forehead from under the soft, wide-brimmed hat, his summer-blue eyes, steely and somber. Willie and Mogie were beside him. At the sight of the two of them, Barbara gasped and stood frozen. Then she moved toward Charlie as if in a dream.

"Charlie, what are you doing here?" she choked out, happy tears splashing over her cheeks like a summer shower. She stumbled into his arms and he hugged her tightly. Then he held her away from him stiffly.

"Barbara, I can't move to Georgia. Even if . . . but if you want to go back, I won't stop you." His voice was low and very sad.

With a pang, Barbara knew he had received her letter. Then she stepped back and burst into a flood of tears.

CHAPTER 25

*B*arbara noticed the shadows in Charlie's eyes, and then she looked at Willie. He stood apart, his gaze fixed on the ground, Mogie wiggling in his arms. *Something is wrong!* she thought. Why had they come here to the stage stop? Why did they behave almost like strangers? She knew the pony express now delivered mail from Junction City, but surely this wasn't why they were here.

She opened her mouth, then closed it again, not knowing what to say and perturbed at their silence. In the background, she was aware of Uncle Daniel slinging Bitsy's bags into the wagon and saw him follow her into the station.

Barbara laid a hand placatively on Charlie's shoulders. "I . . . I'm sorry, but I can't help out with buying the ranch after all. You see, I . . . we . . . "

Charlie nodded slightly. "I got your letter . . . about living in Georgia. I hope you won't regret leaving there." Then grabbing her tightly, he added, "But I've missed you something fierce!"

She nuzzled her face against his broad shoulders that smelled of horses and sweat and all the sweet prairie smells rolled into one. Pushing herself away, she reached out for Willie's damp, awkward hug.

"Willie, you've grown two more inches while I was gone!"

she cried and he grinned sheepishly. "But why did you leave the ranch to come here? Did you know I'd be on this stage?"

"We just happened to . . . be here when your Uncle Daniel received the wire from Bitsy. I've sure missed you, Barbara. Uh, I hope you'll be happy on your own land." Willie turned and looked at Charlie again. Again she sensed something was wrong.

With a sharp intake of breath, she said, "Oh, but this is what I've been trying to tell you. I had to come back, even without the money to buy the ranch! It was either live on the plantation, or release all claim to it. I chose our ranch."

Willie shot a glance at Charlie, then snorted, "What ranch?"

"Why, our ranch, of course! Please forgive me for wanting to move back to Atlanta. That was stupid of me. But the soddy was so insufferably lonely, and back home there were all those familiar faces. I admit I got carried away. I was selfish, but I know now I can never go back there to live.

"You see, if we want to raise our son on the ranch, I'd better get back there and do my share to make it happen. Maybe Aggie can help hem diapers and Mame Probst can be there to deliver him, if there's no doctor." Her words came out in a rush.

Charlie looked startled, and Willie spun around quickly at her words.

"What . . . what are you saying?" Charlie stared at her, an incredible look in his blue eyes.

"Charlie . . ." she leaned against his chest again. "It's true; it's true. We . . . we're going to have a baby, a son, I hope. Lots of sons. We need them to help with the ranch, you know. Like you said."

For a moment Charlie stared at her and it was apparent that thoughts were spinning in his head. He seemed rather breathless with the news. Barbara turned to look at Willie again, then Charlie gently turned her back to face him.

"Barbara," his voice was low, "I know how upset you were when Eva Mae lost her baby, and how desperately lonely you were, and I can't blame you if you didn't want to come back here. So you don't know how happy I am about . . . about all of this. But as for the ranch—"

"What about our ranch? Tell me!" She stared at them both. "What is it you're not telling me? And how come you just happened to be here when the stage pulled in?"

"We . . . don't have it any more. What happened there two weeks ago . . ." he paused awkwardly.

Charlie and Willie looked at each other. Then Charlie took her into his arms and for a long time he held her close. She could feel his heart pounding in his chest as he laid his warm lips against her cheek.

"Oh, Barbara, Barbara! Two weeks ago, soldiers from Fort Larned rushed into our yard to warn us that the Kiowas and Cheyennes were rampaging across Western Kansas. They'd skirmished along the Smoky Hill for months. Now they were storming down the Trail, killing settlers and burning everything in their path. The Parkers, the McNeers and the Evans jumped into their wagons and fled, leaving everything behind. Willie and I, we threw the most necessary things and some food into a couple of sacks and hurried away. We left none too soon. When we looked back, we saw the Indians thundering up far behind in a cloud of dust and moments later our little place was in flames. They must've driven off the stock first. There's nothing left, Barbara. *Nothing!*"

She drew back in shock. "Oh . . ." Her voice stuck in her throat. The little soddy, gone? Her quilts and featherbeds, the topsy stove, the sampler, and the little God's Acre with the two tiny graves? She swallowed hard. Nothing? It couldn't be!

Then she squared her shoulders. "But I still have . . . the two of you," she whispered with a catch in her throat.

Charlie looked at her intently. "Don't you understand, Barbara? It means . . . we have to start from scratch. You asked how we happened to be here. Well, my darling, I'm working here on the ranch and Willie's helping Mollie, bringing in wood, carrying water and giving a hand in the kitchen. We have a shack which doesn't even have a floor, a little ways down the road. And now you say there's to be a baby? Barbara, don't get me wrong, but I'm not sure what we'll do. I never thought it would come to this. You, coming from a plantation and being forced to live in a shack without a floor!" He shook his head. "I could never ask you to do that. I won't blame you if you want to go back to Georgia."

Barbara's lips felt dry with fear, or was it anger or panic? Her luminous eyes widened with realization. She stroked Charlie's arm gently.

"Charlie, don't you see? That's why I came back . . . because I love you . . . and because I want us to bring up our children here. We'll start over. But whatever happens, we're together, with God to lead us. That's what really matters."

Uncle Daniel came out of the station toward them. Barbara was sure he knew everything.

"It's too bad you had to come back to this, Barbara," he said in his strong, firm voice. "But Lank tells me that the government is planning to retaliate. Congress has asked for treaties to eliminate the Indian menace. There's to be a massive counterattack to drive the Indians to the reservations next spring. It seems they blame the white settlers for killing their buffalo, so they're out for revenge. In a way, you can't blame them. But we've been relatively safe over here. It's mostly the Plains settlers in the West that are being attacked. They're especially vicious along the Smoky Hill River Valley. Charlie's wise in helping on the ranch for now. The Lord's protected you this past year out West. For that we're very grateful."

"I was almost angry enough to join the soldiers myself, except for Willie," Charlie said. "I couldn't leave him. I thought if you were safe in Atlanta—"

"But I came back, Charlie! And wherever you go, I will go. I promised that when we were married! Suddenly I knew that's what I wanted . . . that I could never go back to my old life. I'm just sorry I couldn't bring you the money I'd hoped."

"Hang the money," he burst out. "I didn't marry you for money, but for the love I have for you. I want only what will make you happy. But I never dreamed it would be a shanty without a floor! And now, if there's to be a baby . . ."

Barbara shook her head, still struggling to believe Charlie's words. She could fix it up, with some help. She'd done it before to their soddy. It had been crude, but it was quite cozy with Mame's help . . . Mame! The name slammed into her head.

"What about Mame and Henry Probst? What's happened to them? Did they . . . get away?"

Charlie lowered his gaze. "We got word from the last eastbound stage that the Indians killed Henry. But Mame escaped."

Willie added. "You know how she always knew what she was doin'. She's safe at Fort Larned now, prob'ly bossin' the cook and changin' the fort's muzzle holes around! Like you said, Barbara, she's always been as gritty as a sandbar and snappy as a turtle."

"Mame, bless her dear heart," Barbara murmured. "I thought I'd never say this, but I'm going to miss her. And poor, good-hearted Henry. To think we'll never hear his German accent again." She paused. "Do you think he ever asked Jesus into his life? Mame was quite concerned about his soul. Why didn't I do more? Why didn't I talk to him about the Lord? First, it was Liz Harnish. And then Henry! I promised I'd make my life count."

She sagged wearily against Charlie, for she felt tired and sick again.

Charlie led her to the crude bench in front of the stage stop and seated her there. He sat down beside her, drew off her bonnet and stroked back her unruly hair.

The sun had set and the afterglow darkened to purple. The sky and prairie along the winding Cottonwood River, and the tall trees in the deepening shadows were shrouded in lavender mist.

Uncle Daniel came toward them, twirling his hat in his hands. "Barbara," he said in his strong, confident voice. "I know you and Charlie have been a blessing to the little Pawnee Rock settlement, and I'm sorry it had to end so abruptly. But God has used you in many ways. And Bitsy tells me how kind you were to Widow Potter. You shared your faith in Christ with her. The Lord isn't through with you yet! Your life is just beginning."

"But I've been so stupid—"

Bitsy pushed herself in front of her father and said with a sniff, "Barbie, sometimes I felt like wringing your neck because you were so utterly decent to that woman," she chirked. "But that's one of the things I like about you. No matter how grim things are, you've got the stuff to make it."

"I almost didn't. I was ready to chuck it all and stay in Georgia!"

"Thank God you didn't!" Bitsy snorted. "See you Thanksgiving? Remember, Merritt's coming!" She hugged Barbara and hopped on the wagon. Minutes later Uncle Daniel clucked to Prince and Dolly and the wagon lumbered toward the East.

"I'll miss my cousin," Barbara murmured, wiping her eyes. "She kept life from getting dull, although she bossed me around something fierce!"

Charlie grinned. "Well, you didn't have Mame around for that. But Bitsy will do fine. She'll soon be in her own bed again. And it's time to get you to bed, too. You must be exhausted. Come, my darling. Let's go to our little shanty."

"Wait." She placed a hand on his arm. "Charlie, I know you've had to give up your dream for your ranch with the way things have turned out. But I'll always believe that some day you'll have it, even if I couldn't help."

He wagged his head. "I still can't believe we're going to have a baby. To tell the truth, Barbara," he said, "I realize now that our claim wasn't good ranch land. Still, if the Lord wills, in His own time and place, we'll begin again. Once the Indians have been driven back and we've saved some money, I have plans of starting a ranch south of Fort Harker. A new settlement is springing up around Ellsworth and they tell me it's good cattle country. Already there are several ranches. What with the Kansas-Missouri tracks being laid, cattle will be driven from Texas to Abilene to be shipped to eastern markets. The future looks promising and I want so much for you to share it with me! When your letter came . . . well, I was heartbroken. But the Lord will open doors for us if we keep trusting Him."

"He's already begun, Charlie. We'll have our own ranch hands to help in time!" she said with a tired laugh.

"Yes. Meanwhile, we'll have to stay here at the ranch and wait until God tells us it's time to move on."

Time to move on. The very words that had followed her these past weeks. She'd learned so much about faith and trust over the past months.

Charlie took her in his arms again and gently held her close and she knew he was happy. The nightmare of the last few weeks was over.

"Yeah," Willie said, scooping up Mogie. "It's gotta be a heap more excitin' than ol' Atlanta, pickin' cotton. Barbara, I'm glad you came to your senses and decided to have your baby here on the prairie, where he belongs."

"So am I," she said drowsily. "Look!" she cried suddenly glancing upward. "The yellow cowslip, prairie moon's tiptoeing into the sky. I think it's saying 'Welcome home'."

"Amen," Charlie whispered against her cheek. "Amen!"